YOUNG MISS JOSIE DELANEY,

DETECTIVE

Books by Mary Malone

THIS WAS BRIDGET

THREE WISHES FOR SARAH

HERE'S HOWIE

DEENIE'S COAT

DEENIE'S WAY

YOUNG MISS JOSIE DELANEY, DETECTIVE

Young *Miss Josie Delaney,*

DETECTIVE

by Mary Malone

Illustrated by Rachel S. Horne

 ────────────────────

DODD, MEAD & COMPANY

NEW YORK

Contents

1

The New Family

Josie Delaney supposed that if she were one of the old inhabitants of Delaware Avenue in Bampton, she would be curious, too. She would be standing out on her porch, like that woman across the street, shading her eyes from the sun in order to peer better at the moving van and its contents. "Hub City Express," the vehicle announced in big letters on its side. "Movers of Fine Furniture." Or maybe she would be leaning on a broom, as two other women across the street were doing, watching the new arrivals, and probably forming opinions.

Josie, who was waiting beside the van in front of the house which was to be her family's home now, brightened as she caught sight of another "old inhabitant" approaching, looking interested also in the newcomers to Delaware Avenue. This was a girl around her own age, twelve, and Josie decided she wouldn't mind at all being like *her*. Blonde, blue-eyed and pink-cheeked, she reminded Josie of the girl in the old calendar picture the Delaneys had always tacked up in the kitchen, no matter where they moved.

"Hello!" she called out gaily. "I'm Josie Delaney. What's your name?" The girl smiled, but, before she could answer the question, Josie continued, "I knew it!"

The other's eyes grew round in surprise. "Knew what?" she asked.

"I just knew you'd have perfect teeth—besides everything else!"

The girl giggled. "For heaven's sake!" she exclaimed, eying Josie admiringly in turn.

Josie decided that she was going to like this new neighbor. She hoped they would be good friends. "What's your name?" she inquired again.

"Eleanor. Eleanor Manning. Are *you* moving here?"

Josie sighed. Of course! This was the kind of girl who would be named something pretty and soft like "Eleanor." Just as *she,* tanned, thin (she refused to think of herself as skinny, although her two brothers didn't mind calling her that), lank-haired and plain, would be "Josie."

Well, she reflected, she could remedy the name business somewhat by presenting her new acquaintance with one of her calling cards.

"Come on in," she invited. "Oh, yes, I'm moving into this house with my family."

Eleanor responded eagerly, and she and Josie picked their way around the piled-up boxes and furniture waiting on the porch.

Eleanor seemed as happy as Josie was to discover a

friend, and the newcomer soon found out why. The pretty blond girl was bursting to explain. She could hardly believe her eyes, she said, when she saw the welcome sight on Delaware Avenue today. She had walked around to the front of her house as she'd done every morning since school closed, two weeks ago, wondering how to occupy herself. She had finished her daily dusting, minded her little cousin Jimmy for an hour, and finally been told by her grandmother that she could go out and play.

That would be fine, Eleanor continued, if there was anyone to play with. The East Bampton Playground wouldn't open until one o'clock. Besides, as Eleanor had discovered, most of the playground girls of her age came already provided with companions. What she longed for was a very special girl friend on her own street. But Delaware Avenue seemed to be running out of children. Even Gramma and her aunt Marie, Mrs. Hogan, had noticed it. The Manning youngsters were about the only ones left—Eleanor herself, her fifteen-year-old brother John Edward, and the little nephew.

"Your fifteen-year-old brother?" Josie interposed at this point.

"Yes, John Edward," Eleanor repeated, and continued to explain that she never did get to look *down* Delaware Avenue today, because six houses up, looming halfway across the street as it stood backed up to the porch, she had seen that large moving van!

"I didn't think it was possible," Eleanor exclaimed, "a

family really taking this old house that's been empty for years, ever since the Ryans moved away! Gramma says it's become so ramshackle now that no respectable family— *Oops!"* She stopped and covered her mouth with her hand. "I'm sorry—I didn't mean—"

Josie smiled. "Don't worry."

She had noticed the broken windows and sagging steps, of course, and so had her mother, when they had come around a few days ago to look over the house. But they had lived in worse places, as Josie very well knew.

"It seems like a very nice neighborhood," she said, to make Eleanor feel better.

"Oh, yes!" agreed the other girl quickly. "And it's on a corner—your house, I mean. I think it's nice to live in a corner house, don't you? Delaware and Willow is your address."

"Delaware and Willow," Josie repeated. "Pretty names." This was a big improvement over Dock Street and Beakes Street, and some of the other addresses her family had known.

She saw Eleanor watching the moving men carry in the shabby sofa with springs poking out from the bottom, and then the old round table.

"That's just like Mrs. O'Toole's dining-room table," Eleanor remarked, "except that hers is—" She stopped, looking a little confused, and gulped. "Hers is—shinier."

Josie grinned. "I'll bet it isn't all scratched like ours," she said cheerfully. She was sure Eleanor thought all the Delaneys' possessions were pretty shabby and worn. She looked at the things the men were bringing in—the beds, chairs, boxes of dishes and pots and pans—with a critical eye.

"All of our furniture is beat up," she continued. "We've moved a lot, you see. And besides, I have two regular demons for brothers. Here they come now," she added as two small boys clattered down the stairs and ran straight into the moving van, backed up to the front door.

She and Eleanor watched, and in a moment saw the boys reappear, lugging a large and battered-looking rocking horse.

Josie stamped her foot and called, "Alexander! Baby Frank! Leave that disgusting thing outside."

Alexander, who was eight, and Baby Frank, six, looked very much alike, with ragged, sun-streaked hair and sharp features. Both faces turned now to Josie, and she wasn't surprised to see they wore almost identical innocent smiles. But the small brothers continued to maneuver the rocking horse through the front door of the house.

"Get out of the way, Jo," Alexander said calmly. To Eleanor he remarked, "I beg your pardon."

Josie shrugged. She didn't want to make a scene in front of her new friend, who was staring in fascination at the boys. And, of course, the rocking horse wasn't any shabbier than the furniture being moved into the house. In fact, Josie had to admit that, in spite of the scratches and dents, Prancer, as the boys had affectionately named the toy, looked rather elegant. In his old-fashioned way, he was the picture of equine pride—head up, nostrils flaring, chest swelling, tail flowing. Although he capered only on wooden rockers, Josie knew that the boys, in imagination, traveled the world over on him.

But a stranger wouldn't know all that, so Josie felt she had to explain. "They insist on dragging that old thing with them every time we move," she said, as she stepped out of the way.

Eleanor nodded. "What interesting-looking boys," she remarked politely. "They have very unusual names, too."

"That reminds me," Josie said. "I wanted to show you something. Come on out here—I suppose this would be the dining room, if we had any suitable furniture," she remarked as she escorted Eleanor to the room between the parlor and the kitchen. "Anyhow," she continued, returning to the subject of the rocking horse, "I'll fix Alexander and B. F. I'll put that old rackety thing out for trash the first chance I get—while they're in bed or something." After all, she told herself, it was time the boys outgrew such a childish plaything.

Eleanor looked alarmed. "Won't they be mad? I don't think I'd want either Alexander or Baby Frank to be—annoyed—at me. They look—" She hesitated.

Josie grinned. Her new friend was having a hard time trying to be diplomatic about the Delaneys. "Those two will try anything that comes into their heads—but I'm a match for them!"

"Well, you *are* older," Eleanor murmured, and looked questioningly at Josie.

"Surely, I am. I'd have to be, to cope with them. I'm the same age as you are—twelve."

"Is that all?" Eleanor was clearly surprised. "You dress older." She examined Josie's costume—her best one, worn especially for moving day. The red dress wasn't very fresh by now, but it did have that wide belt, nipping it in at the waist. And the straw slippers were decidedly chic, Josie herself thought, taking delight in the way they flip-flopped with every step she took.

Eleanor added wistfully, "I wish *I* could go without stockings. I hate these bobby socks. You know," she exclaimed suddenly, "I think I have a dress something like yours! I used to wear it. It's too short now, but maybe I could let down the hem—and I might even find a wide belt to go with it." She turned as if to leave.

"Don't go!" cried Josie, and ran over to a box she knew held her things. She rummaged through it and found one of her cards. "Here!"

She was glad to see that Eleanor looked impressed as she read aloud what was printed on the card. "Miss Josie Delaney, Authoress."

"My goodness!" Eleanor gasped. "You are a—an—authoress?"

"Positively," Josie replied, and couldn't help beaming at her new friend's awe-stricken expression. "I had a poem printed in *Children's Life*. I'll show you."

It was a little harder to find the magazine she sought among the boxes and bursting bags that had been set down just anyway in the dining room. Finally, she found what she wanted and offered it to Eleanor. "See. *The Seasons,* by Josie Delaney."

Eleanor read the four-line poem and before she could remark on the signature, "Josie Delaney, Age 10," the author herself hastened to explain. "I wish they hadn't put my age there. That was two years ago, and I haven't been able to think up another poem since."

"You probably don't have time," Eleanor responded generously. "Are you in charge of this house? I mean—do you have any—"

"You're more polite than most other people, Eleanor. Don't worry. I'm used to questions. There's something about our family that brings out all the questions. Here goes, then. My mother is working at the telephone office. She's a long-distance operator. We've moved around a lot, as I told you, so she said there wasn't anything I couldn't take care of. Besides, she didn't want to lose a day's pay." Josie added cheerfully, "We never seem to have enough money."

Eleanor nodded. "Is your father working, too?"

"No, he's away," Josie replied. She suddenly looked very unhappy. "He was very sick, but now he's getting better—in a sanatorium." It still hurt so deeply to talk about her father's illness and the separation from his devoted family as a result, so she changed the subject. "Imagine having a tree all our own in the back yard!" She indicated the stunted little tree that grew beside the kitchen door. "Isn't it just gorgeous?" She decided to

*"Imagine having a tree all our own in the back yard! Isn't it gor-
geous?" She decided to overlook the weeds.*

overlook—for now—the rampant growth of weeds in the yard.

"Apples grow on that tree, too," Eleanor informed her. "In the fall."

"Oh! That's even more gorgeous. Think of all the applesauce I can make!"

"Applesauce! Do we have any? I just feel like some," Alexander declared as he and Baby Frank appeared again, dragging boxes this time, after having carefully placed their rocking horse in a corner of the dining room.

"Your ant colony?" Josie demanded, as she recognized one of the boxes. "And don't tell me you have your turtle there, too!"

"*Beep, beep!*" called out Baby Frank, speeding by on his tricycle. "The moving men are almost ready to leave, Jo."

"They said they'd give us a ride downtown," Alexander said, hurriedly stacking his possessions next to the rocking horse. "Frank, put the tricycle here on the other side of Prancer. There! We're finished, Jo. Can we go with the men?"

"How will you get back?" Josie asked.

"Walk," responded Alexander promptly. "Maybe we'll go over to the telephone office and visit Mom."

"What time is it?" Josie suddenly remembered her duties.

"Almost twelve o'clock," said Eleanor, looking at her wrist watch.

She has to have a wrist watch, too, Josie thought, and

wondered whether to be envious. She decided not to be. I'm better dressed, she told herself. She supposed some people would even dispute that point, preferring Eleanor's starched and scrubbed appearance to her own rather disheveled even if smart look. But Eleanor's dress *was* a little babyish, Josie decided, and those bobby socks!

"I should be getting lunch," she said aloud.

"If it's baked beans again, we don't want any," Alexander announced. "Besides, we haven't time. The men are waiting."

"I want a hot dog when we get downtown," Baby Frank piped up. "Give us a quarter, Jo. Two hot dogs and a glass of root beer—with two straws."

"I guess it would be worth it—to get rid of you," Josie remarked, pretending scorn, but secretly rather envying her little brothers' fun. *She* would like to hop a ride in the moving truck, too, and have a hot dog and root beer in the five-and-ten, and wander around downtown the rest of the day. For a wild moment, she thought of proposing such an excursion to Eleanor.

But a quick glance at the demure face and spotless dress of the other girl convinced her that Eleanor was not the type to do things on the spur of the moment.

"Hurry up, Jo," Alexander urged, and as soon as Josie had fished out a quarter from her *very* chic—she thought —patent-leather handbag, he and Baby Frank whipped out of the house and into the moving van.

In a few moments, the girls heard the rattle of the van as it pulled away from the house, and saw it lumber down the road with Alexander and Baby Frank waving from the back of it.

Eleanor looked as if she wanted to ask some questions, as curiosity struggled with politeness on her expressive face. "Maybe they'll get lost downtown," was all she said, though.

Josie shook her head. "They know their way around." She grinned. "They always turn up at suppertime. Which reminds me. I have to go to the store sometime and get hamburger for supper."

"Are *you* going to cook supper?" Eleanor wanted to know.

"Of course. And before that, I'm going to clean this house—*after* I pick out my bedroom. My mother said I could have first choice. Oh, isn't this gorgeous? A big house like this and *three* bedrooms!"

Eleanor seemed disappointed. "I thought maybe you could come over to my house this afternoon. But if you have to do all that—"

"I can come!" Josie exclaimed quickly. "I'll tidy up first and have everything in place before my mother gets here. Then I'll stop at your house on my way to the store."

"I don't see how you can straighten up all these rooms in such a short time," Eleanor said doubtfully.

"With the boys out of the way, I'll sail through in no time. You'll see. Or maybe you could—" It was on the tip of Josie's tongue to offer Eleanor a chance to help her with the cleaning. But second thoughts stopped her. Not in that spick-and-span dress. Eleanor's family would probably be very upset if she arrived home dirty and rumpled. From the way her new friend spoke and looked, Josie had formed an opinion of the Manning family. They were just-so—their house and clothes and everything. There wouldn't be any dust, or broken windowpanes or peeling wallpaper, all of which were very easy to point out here. She saw these things, just as well as Eleanor did, but she had determined to rise above them. She'd had lots of practice doing *that*.

"This place is simply gorgeous," she repeated firmly, to reassure herself. She knew she used the word *gorgeous* quite a bit, but she just couldn't help it. She'd always had spells of infatuation with certain words and used them all the time—at least for a month or so. Until a new word caught her fancy. Only last night, Mom had said, half in amusement and half in exasperation, "Josie, if you use that word *gorgeous* once more, I shall scream!"

"I'll have to go home now," Eleanor said. "My grandmother will be wondering about me."

"My goodness!" Josie protested. "Doesn't she realize that you're twelve years old and big enough to take care of yourself?"

"It isn't that," Eleanor explained, looking a little uncomfortable, as if Josie made her seem too young. "But we'll be having lunch and—"

Josie interrupted swiftly. "Oh, maybe I can go to your house for lunch—" Then, just as swiftly, when Eleanor hesitated, "No!" she declared. "Better to go over later, after you've prepared your family for me." She grinned.

Eleanor left, smiling, after telling Josie just where her house was.

Josie wondered, as she watched the other girl walking sedately down the street, if her friend was going to be able to explain the Delaneys—Alexander, Baby Frank, Josie herself—to that very particular family. She fervently hoped so, because she thought Eleanor was one of the nicest girls she'd ever met. It would be fine to be friends with her.

Josie decided that she was going to try like anything to be sensible and proper, too, so as not to shock Eleanor or her family.

She gave Prancer a push as she went by, and he rocked gently, as if nodding in approval of her decision.

2

Summer Plans

After Eleanor left, Josie quickly set the house to rights. The moving men had put the heavy pieces of furniture in place, and the Delaneys really did not own much more than bare essentials. So Josie merely sorted out the miscellaneous collection of boxes and bags, swept the floors, and wiped all the kitchen surfaces with a strong solution of ammonia and water. Her mother would be pleased, when she came home, if that clean smell met her at the door.

Then Josie scrubbed herself—at least where it showed—cinched her belt a little tighter, set her straw hat firmly on her head, and pulled on an old pair of long kid gloves that had belonged to her mother. She felt that she would make a better impression on Eleanor's family if she were dressed properly when she went to visit.

She found Eleanor's house easily—it was only a block away on Delaware Avenue—and noted how spotless were the white marble steps leading to the front door, how glistening the windowpanes, and how swept of all foreign objects the red-brick pavement in front.

She climbed the steps and was about to press the doorbell when voices coming from within the house caught her attention. They were not loud voices, but it was very quiet on the street just then, and Josie could hear distinctly.

"A fine job of cleaning will have to be done there," somebody said. It sounded like an older woman, probably Eleanor's grandmother, Josie thought.

"I wonder if the boys might be playmates for little Jimmy," a younger-sounding person said. This was the aunt, Josie decided.

Then came a snort and the husky tones of a growing boy—John Edward. "You'd better inspect those fellows first, Aunt Marie. They've been in a fight already."

"Were they hurt?" Eleanor asked.

Josie smiled to herself as John Edward replied, "They might have hurt their fists a little—pounding on Tom Willis. But he deserved it. He made fun of their haircuts, and they tore into him like wildcats."

Josie thought it was time for her to make an entrance. She rang the bell.

The voices stopped.

She peered in through the screen door and saw Eleanor hurrying toward her down a long, dim hallway. Heavens, what a gorgeous home this was, Josie thought. Carpets, and pictures on the wall, and pretty lamps, and flowers—

"How do you do? I am Miss Josie Delaney."

there was a big bowl of yellow roses on a table just inside the door.

Eleanor looked surprised. "Why, you're all dressed up," she said, staring at Josie's hat and gloves.

Two women followed Eleanor to the door. They were both smiling pleasantly. A slam of the back door told Josie that the boy had fled.

"Is this your friend, Eleanor?" the older woman—it was the grandmother, of course—asked. "Invite her in, child."

Josie responded quickly as Eleanor opened the door. "How do you do? I am Miss Josie Delaney. You must be Eleanor's grandmother and you're her aunt. What a lovely, lovely home you have!"

"Thank you," said Aunt Marie, exchanging an amused glance with the older lady. "Won't you come in here and sit down and take off your hat?" she asked, leading the way to the pretty little parlor overlooking Delaware Avenue.

Josie laid her hat, gloves, and pocketbook on a chair and settled back to enjoy herself. "I've done a lot of work since you left, Eleanor. I cleaned the house from top to bottom, arranged all the furniture where it belongs, and—"

Eleanor, looking astounded, broke in, "Oh, but how could you? In such a short time, I mean?"

"There was nobody to stop me, with the boys out of the way," replied Josie airily.

"Did you know they were in a fight?" Eleanor inquired.

"No," said Josie briefly, and didn't ask any questions. She wasn't worried about the boys, knowing very well that they could take care of themselves. Besides, she had overheard the Mannings' conversation.

Eleanor's grandmother asked where the Delaneys had lived before, and this was all that was needed to start Josie on a lively account of her family's wanderings. Before coming to Delaware Avenue, they had lived in South Bampton, in several different houses, and before that, in Brooklyn. She saw that Eleanor's relatives were enjoying the conversation, so she expanded, and, as usual, exaggerated, just a little. She'd lost count of all the schools she had attended, she said. Even Baby Frank had gone to three different kindergartens in the last year.

"How about the older boy—Alexander, is it?" Aunt Marie asked.

"Alessandro, really," Josie explained. "My mother had just finished reading *Ramona* when he was born. But nobody can ever get it straight, so we call him Alexander." She added matter-of-factly, "He's a genius."

"Really?" murmured Aunt Marie.

Eleanor seemed awe-stricken. "A genius and an authoress in one family!" she marveled, and Josie enlarged still more.

"He can sing, play the piano, paint pictures, and stuff dead animals," she continued.

"Glory be!" Gramma exclaimed. "Dead animals, did you say?"

"Rabbits and squirrels and things like that," Josie explained. "When we lived in the country, he had quite a lot of practice."

"But, Josie," protested Eleanor. It was plain to see that she was still several steps behind. "I didn't see any piano in your house."

Fortunately, Josie was saved from further explanations by Aunt Marie. "Will you have some lemonade and cookies?" she asked.

"Positively, thank you." Josie beamed. "I'd love some." She would, too, she told herself, because she hadn't bothered about lunch. "Now, Eleanor," she urged as Aunt Marie left to prepare the refreshments. "Tell me all about the possibilities of this neighborhood. What do you do for fun?"

"Why—nothing much," Eleanor acknowledged, frowning in thought. "There's the playground—"

"Good!" pronounced Josie. "Is there a swimming pool?"

"Downtown somewhere, I guess," Eleanor answered. "I don't know just where—"

"We'll find it," promised Josie. "Any tennis courts nearby?"

"Oh, no, I don't think so. Can you play tennis?"

"Anybody can. We'll have to find rackets. How about your big brother? Would he have one?"

"No, he only plays baseball in the summer."

"Never mind. We'll find somebody who owns a tennis racket. We'll visit the library, too. And the museum. Maybe the Y has art classes. There must be a cooking school somewhere. So tomorrow we'll start out early and see what happens. That is, if your grandmother agrees."

She turned to Gramma, who had been listening to all this in amused silence.

Eleanor looked dazed, contemplating the sudden rash of summer activities. "My goodness," she said, "only yesterday I had nothing to do. And now today—" She left her sentence unfinished, but Josie understood her meaning and smiled at her new friend.

"We'll have lots of fun," she declared.

Aunt Marie returned to the parlor with a tray holding a frosty pitcher of lemonade, sparkling glasses, and a plate piled high with chocolate cookies. After everybody had been served, and the first draught of lemonade had quenched the hot afternoon's thirst, Josie continued to answer questions, while hungrily eating cookies. She was very careful not to talk with her mouth full, however.

"Now tell me some more about yourself," she directed Eleanor finally. "Why do you live with your grandmother and aunt, instead of your mother and father?"

"My Uncle James, too," Eleanor added, and continued, in answer to Josie's question, "because my mother and father are dead."

Aunt Marie explained, "She was only a baby when she lost her parents." She placed her hand on Eleanor's protectively.

Privately, Josie thought they still treated Eleanor somewhat like a baby. She decided to investigate a more interesting aspect of her friend's family. "How about your brother?" she asked. "Your older brother?"

"John Edward's my only brother," Eleanor replied. "But he doesn't like girls."

"Is he cute?" Josie persisted.

Eleanor shrugged. "I don't know. He's my *brother.*"

"Bring him over with you to visit us tomorrow," Josie invited. "We'll have a picnic lunch in the back yard."

"He won't come," Eleanor warned.

"Boys always like picnics," Josie asserted.

After the two women had gone back to their work, she still visited for nearly an hour, learning more about Eleanor's family, then remarked it was time to leave. "I have to do some shopping," she explained, consulting a list she took from her pocketbook. "Hamburger. Potato chips. Soda. That'll do it, I guess." She stuffed the paper back into her bag.

"Is that what you're going to have for supper?" Eleanor asked.

Josie nodded. "It's the easiest thing to prepare," she said. "I just didn't have time to do any cooking today."

She rose from the sofa, put on her hat and gloves, then went to the door of the kitchen, where she heard the voices of Gramma and Aunt Marie. "Thank you for a lovely time—" She started to say "Mrs. Manning and Mrs. Hogan," but quickly changed her mind. "Gramma and Aunt Marie," she ended.

Both women came out to say good-by. "Come again," they invited warmly, and Josie promised she would.

As she skipped down the front steps, she heard Gramma comment, "She's a marvel, that one!"

Josie smiled to herself. She hoped Eleanor's family would continue to think well of her. She herself would try to be careful, and behave in a more lady-like way, and not exaggerate so much, and even be nicer to her little brothers—maybe.

3

Taking Possession

Josie called for her new friend bright and early the next morning. She decided she would stay outside while Eleanor arranged matters with her family.

While she was waiting, a boy bolted out of the house, nodded curtly to her, and hurried away. Josie looked after him with interest. He was John Edward, of course, and he *was* cute, she thought, although he looked as if he'd punch anyone who told him so. She agreed with Eleanor—reluctantly—that John Edward wasn't likely to show up for a picnic lunch in the Delaneys' back yard.

Even Eleanor seemed to be having a little difficulty about coming. Josie heard her asking her aunt for permission.

"But if you're going for *lunch,* why so early?" Aunt Marie wanted to know. "It's only nine o'clock."

"We have so many things to do today," Eleanor explained. "We're going downtown, I think, and find out about—oh, you know, what Josie said—tennis and swimming, and cooking school, and all."

"You couldn't possibly do everything she suggested," Aunt Marie continued. "What do you think, Mother? Do you suppose they'll get in any trouble? That Josie—"

Josie strained to catch the grandmother's reply, almost lost in a clatter of dishes. She relaxed when she heard, "They'll be all right. Josie struck me as a young lady well able to take care of herself. And Eleanor knows how to behave. As soon as her work here is done, she may go."

"It is all done, Gramma," Eleanor responded eagerly. "I made the beds and dusted upstairs and tied up the newspapers for the garbage and swept the porch and—"

"All right! All right!" Gramma laughed. "It seems that the chores are going to be done early from now on."

Eleanor slipped out soon after that, wearing a red dress that was too short for her. "Why are you wearing that old thing?" Gramma called after her.

"This is the nearest thing to yours I could find," she explained to Josie, who nodded in approval.

At the Delaneys', the girls found that the little boys had staked off their new property and were patrolling it with make-believe rifles. Because the house was on a corner, there was the side as well as the downtrodden front lawn to protect. Barricades made of sticks and crates had been set up, and the boys challenged anyone who attempted to pass.

"Friend or foe?" Alexander demanded of Eleanor as

the girls approached from the front. Baby Frank was guarding the side.

"You know who I am!" Eleanor said.

"She's with me, of course," Josie explained.

"Friend or foe?" Alexander insisted. "You have to say."

"Oh, go ahead, Eleanor," Josie advised. "Humor them."

"Friend," Eleanor said.

"Pass," directed Alexander, removing the stick that had barred the way. "The password for today is 'Mononga-hela.' Baby Frank will let you through if you say it."

"She's not going through. She's staying," Josie said, "for lunch."

Alexander grinned. "We're having hot dogs and cream soda, aren't we, Jo?"

Two big boys began to cross the street. Alexander's expression quickly changed. He looked quite threatening. "Stop!" he ordered, pointing his rifle as the boys headed toward the short cut which disfigured the Delaneys' front yard.

"What's the big idea?" one boy demanded. "We've always cut across this yard."

Yes, you and the whole neighborhood, I'll bet, Josie thought.

"Not any more," declared Alexander. "Now you need to know the password."

Grinning, the boys stopped. Then they noticed Eleanor. "What are *you* doing here?" one of them asked.

"These are my friends," she answered, and to Alex-

ander she said, "I know them. Mike Foley and Albert Schmidt."

Alexander ignored this introduction and continued to glare.

"Well, well," said the boy Eleanor called Mike. "We'll have to fight our way though."

"Forgot my gun today, too," the other one replied. "Just my luck."

"Bare hands, then," Mike continued, smiling.

"Frank!" Alexander called, without turning around. He kept his rifle fixed on Mike.

"Bringing up reinforcements," Mike murmured. "Afraid we have trouble on our hands, Al."

"Cover *him*," Alexander directed, nodding toward Albert as Baby Frank charged up, his rifle at the ready.

"Say!" exclaimed Albert suddenly, in a different tone. "Aren't you the little demons that beat up Tom Willis?"

Alexander and Baby Frank didn't waste words agreeing or disagreeing. They waited, in the same unfriendly attitude.

"That's right!" Mike declared. "Well, that's different. We'll retreat. Come on, Al." The big boys turned to go around the barricade. "You won't shoot us in the back, will you?" asked Mike.

"You can pass!" called Alexander loudly, lowering his rifle.

"Thanks, sonny." Mike started to pat Baby Frank on the head, then quickly withdrew his hand. "Better not," he told Eleanor and Josie, who were watching. "He might bite."

Josie giggled. "Are they neighbors?" she asked Eleanor as the two older boys walked off and Baby Frank returned to his post.

When Eleanor said the boys were friends of John Edward, Josie was interested. "I wish they had stayed," she said.

"I don't," Eleanor declared. "They tease me."

Josie nodded. "But *you* could annoy *them*, you know. There are lots of ways to get under their skin. Oh, well, some other time, maybe. I'll get our lunch. We'll just carry it out to the yard. Alexander! Can we use your crates for tables and chairs?"

It was hardly ten o'clock yet but the prospect of lunch—the Delaneys had all skipped breakfast—was enough for Alexander and Baby Frank to dismantle their barricades and take them to the yard. Eleanor helped Josie carry out the food.

Josie decided that the hot dogs and potato chips, and the soda to wash them down, tasted good enough to make her—and Eleanor, too, she hoped—forget the weeds, high and scratchy on her bare legs, and the broiling sun.

After lunch, the boys rearranged their defenses and then dragged the rocking horse outside.

Nobody else challenged their occupation of the sidewalk. Josie noticed that people seemed to be staying on the other side of the street.

Contentedly, Alexander and Baby Frank took turns riding and fondling Prancer. They talked to him as if he were human, Josie thought, and smiled knowingly at Eleanor.

"He's a fancy horse," said Eleanor. Josie nodded. The old fellow did have a noble sort of look, and even the bright sun did not diminish the effect.

"Are we going to leave the boys alone?" Eleanor asked as she and Josie started downtown.

"Of course," Josie replied. She added, "They never fight each other. Only outsiders. Two against the world, like. But let's forget about them, now, and enjoy ourselves. Where to, first?"

"There's a swimming pool over on Green Street, John Edward says. About six blocks this way and four that way. Shall we try that?"

"Positively!" Josie declared, using one of her favorite words just then. "Come on!"

4

Names and Addresses

Eleanor and Josie were crossing East End Avenue where trolley tracks bisected the center of the road, when Eleanor suddenly stopped. She looked dismayed.

"Oh, dear!" she exclaimed. "I just remembered. We can't—"

"Come on, get out of the road," Josie advised. "If we can, that is. My feet are sinking in this tar." The sun was hot enough to melt the asphalt, and the two girls could feel the scorching heat of East End Avenue on the soles of their feet, even through their shoes.

Once safely across the street, Eleanor explained. "East End Avenue marks the dividing line between the city and the township."

"What difference does that make?" Josie inquired.

"We're in the township because we live on Delaware Avenue. The Green Street swimming pool is city."

Josie was beginning to grow impatient. It was uncomfortable standing in the blistering sun. She looked longingly across the street, to where a row of stores, shaded by awnings, would provide some relief from the glare. "Well, what if it is?" she asked. "City, township, who cares?"

"Don't you see? If we live in the township, we're not entitled to use the city pool—or tennis court, or library, or anything."

"Who says we're not entitled?" Josie was never impressed by regulations unless she understood the reason. And this didn't seem reasonable.

Eleanor looked puzzled. "I don't know, but I think it's because we don't pay taxes to the city."

"All right," Josie replied. "Let me think."

She was silent for a few moments. . . . Then, "I have it," she announced. "It's very simple. We just give city addresses when they ask us."

"But wouldn't that be wrong?" Eleanor inquired.

Josie shrugged. "Not really. We're not hurting anyone. Don't worry about it," she advised.

"How about names?" Eleanor *was* worried, as Josie could see from the troubled expression on her friend's face.

She nodded. "They should match the addresses. That won't be hard. I can think of quite a few."

Still, Eleanor was disturbed. Of course, she would be, because she was not the adventurous kind, Josie realized, so she tried to bolster her companion. *"Don't worry,* I said. Why is it wrong for poor, underprivileged kids like us to use their crummy old swimming pool? They ought to be *glad* we're willing to come all this way."

Eleanor said nothing.

"I'm really glad you thought of this enough ahead, though," Josie continued, smiling kindly at Eleanor. "It gives us time to think of different names and addresses. Let's see. If it'll make you feel any better, how about using the address of some relative who lives in the city? You must have somebody."

"Gramma's sister—that's my Aunt Winnie—lives on Ewing Street," Eleanor recalled.

"Fine," Josie said encouragingly. "What's her name—her last name? And the number on Ewing Street?"

"Carney. But she lives all alone—"

"What number?" Josie insisted.

"Twelve—I think."

Josie couldn't help pointing out, "It would be better if you *knew*. But they won't check up. They never do. All right, then. You are Eleanor Carney, 12 Ewing Street. Now listen," she went on persuasively. "It isn't wrong. What's to stop you from going to live with your aunt? And wouldn't you be entitled then? So don't be silly," she concluded briskly. "I don't have any relatives, but I know lots of people. I'll take the Johnsons on Monument Street, where we used to live. They have so many kids already, it won't make any difference if one more is added. I'm Josie Johnson, 149 Monument Street." The name pleased her and she repeated, "Josie Johnson. J. J. I like that."

When they arrived at the pool, the girls were ready with their new identities. By this time, Eleanor had been convinced that they were not doing any harm. Then she saw how easy it was—just as Josie said. The young lady in charge at the pool accepted their names and addresses unquestioningly. Josie thought that Eleanor was even beginning to enjoy the adventure. When they left the building, clutching their cards, the officer on duty outside held up traffic for them to cross the street. He was so jovial that Josie asked him how to get to the YWCA. When he said it was just a few blocks away, she proposed going there next.

The bulletin board outside the Y listed several summer activities for children during that summer in the 1920's. There were handicraft classes, dancing instruction, and a junior cooking school which would begin on July 15.

"That's for us," declared Josie, pointing to the last announcement. "I've been to cooking school before. It's fun, and they let you eat whatever you cook."

"Are we entitled?" Eleanor asked.

"Positively—one way or the other. We'll try giving our own names this time."

This turned out to be all right—at first. But the girls hadn't anticipated that a fee was necessary before they could be accepted. The lady at the desk informed them about this after they had registered.

"Two dollars!" Josie exclaimed.

Eleanor stammered, "We—we didn't know—"

Evidently, the pair looked so crushed that the lady took pity on them.

"Well, we do have some scholarships open to poor children—city children, I mean," she amended hastily. "Maybe we can arrange for you to have one of those. Let's see, now." She consulted the list on which she had added their names and addresses. "Oh, I'm sorry. You're not in the city, are you? That's a requirement."

"But we—" began Eleanor. She was stopped by Josie's foot, firmly pressed on hers.

"Never mind," Josie told the lady, assuming a brave smile. "It's all right. Good-by!"

"Of all the luck!" she exclaimed when they were outside. "We could have given our other names and addresses if we'd known. I was afraid you were going to, El. That's why I stepped on your foot."

"I guess cooking school is out for us," Eleanor said wistfully.

"Oh, no," Josie declared coolly. "All we have to do is come back when *that* lady isn't here. She won't be, every day. They're society ladies, you know, and they volunteer for Y work. Tomorrow, a different one will be here. You'll see. So we'll come back then and give our other names."

She looked at Eleanor's watch. "It's one o'clock. What shall we do now?"

"Maybe we'd better go home," answered Eleanor.

Josie made a face. "Already? It's early yet. We could go to the movies, if we had the money." She stood, gazing around, speculating.

Eleanor looked alarmed. "Don't think up any more

ideas, Josie," she begged. "We've done enough for one day."

"But it's too soon to go home," Josie said. Besides, she didn't want to do any more cleaning, and that's about all there was to do at home.

Eleanor shook her head. "Not for me. Come on," she urged. "It'll take a half hour to get back. And I don't want to be away too long. Gramma and Aunt Marie will wonder, if I am. Then I might have to tell them about—you know—signing up under false names."

Josie was exasperated. "They're *not* false names. We didn't take anybody else's name. We just thought of new ones for ourselves."

"Even so," said Eleanor uncomfortably, "I don't think it was right."

Josie was about to argue. Then a closer look at Eleanor's troubled face made her change her mind. "All right," she said reasonably. "We'll go home. Tomorrow's another day."

5

The Rocking Horse

But there was more excitement back home.

When the girls arrived at Josie's house, they found both Alexander and Baby Frank in a highly indignant state. It seemed that while the boys had been lazing away the hot afternoon, taking turns on the rocking horse and at the barricade, not bothering anybody except those few who made the mistake of trying to pass on their side of the street, some man had come by and asked a lot of questions—all about the rocking horse. At the time, they didn't think so much about it, but after the man had left, Alexander became suspicious.

"He sure was newsy," he had said to Baby Frank. He repeated it now, in front of the girls.

"Sure was newsy," echoed Baby Frank.

"What difference does it make to him, where we got Prancer?"

"Yeah," agreed Baby Frank.

"He had some nerve," continued Alexander, working himself up to a frenzy.

"Let's go after him!" Baby Frank cried.

The boys were about to rush off on this mission when Josie grabbed them, one in each hand.

"Stay still!" she commanded sternly. "You're not going anywhere—yet."

She succeeded in holding her two brothers and demanded to know more about the inquisitive man who had been asking about the rocking horse.

"It's peculiar," she said to Eleanor. "Nobody before ever showed the slightest interest in the old thing."

She released the boys. A little more subdued now, they took turns in telling her about their visitor. The man had wanted to know where they had found the horse, if somebody had painted it black, and if it had a certain mark underneath.

"We wouldn't let him look!" Alexander exclaimed.

"He wanted to turn Prancer upside down," Baby Frank said indignantly.

"But why—why?" Josie demanded. "Why did he ask all those questions?"

Alexander shrugged. "He didn't tell us."

"More likely, you didn't give him a chance to explain," Josie said glumly. "I know you two."

She walked over to the rocking horse and examined it more closely than she ever had before. "Maybe there's something about it I didn't appreciate," she admitted. "I just considered it as part of your junk. I was even going to throw it out in the trash. Remember, Eleanor?"

Both boys let out a bellow at this, and Baby Frank ran over to his sister and wrapped himself around her, beating her with his tiny fists.

Laughing, she detached him from her legs. "All right, all right, I just said I was going to. I won't, now— not if somebody else thinks your plaything is so great."

"It has a sad face," Eleanor said, as she, too, looked more carefully at the rocking horse.

"Not *it,*" protested Alexander. *"He. Prancer."*

"Where did it—I mean he—really come from, anyway?" Eleanor asked. "If it isn't a secret," she added politely, looking askance at Baby Frank, who had not relaxed.

"They found it in a junk yard—in South Bampton," Josie explained. "Years ago."

She scratched the horse's paint with her fingernail. Excitedly, she saw a piece flake off and reveal a smooth white surface underneath. "Look!" she cried. "It *has* been painted over! It must have been white before."

"You know what?" Alexander suddenly recalled. "He wanted to know about our mother and father. When could he see them, or something like that."

"Who? The man? What did you tell him?" Josie asked.

"Told him it was none of his business," Alexander answered.

Josie shrugged and made a face at Eleanor. "What little angels my brothers are!" Then of Alexander she demanded, "Why didn't you tell him to come back when Mother is home?"

" 'Cause we don't want him!" Alexander declared.

"He might buy the horse," Josie suggested.

"No!" shrieked Baby Frank. "Don't want him!"

"We could certainly use the money," Josie pointed out.

"No! No! No!" Baby Frank cried.

Alexander said stubbornly, "Nobody gets Prancer."

There was silence for a few minutes.

"Well, I'll have to go," Eleanor said. "See you tomorrow, Josie."

"Positively," Josie replied absently. Then she roused herself, and gave the rocking horse a push. "I'll come over to your house in the morning."

6

Disappearance

The next morning, Josie was awakened by shouts from her brothers. She glanced at the alarm clock and saw that it was only eight-thirty. Too early to get up, she decided, and turned over, pulling the pillow around her head so she couldn't hear the little boys' racket. Her mother had left long ago for the telephone office. Josie was supposed to see to getting breakfast ready for her brothers and herself, and she did. But the time depended on when she felt hungry—or the boys began clamoring for food.

However, she wasn't going to be able to sleep any more this morning, for Alexander and Baby Frank rushed into her room and started to shake her.

"Wake up, Jo!" Alexander shouted.

Baby Frank was sobbing.

"What in the world is the matter with you two?" Josie demanded, sitting up.

"Prancer is gone! Somebody stole him!" Alexander exclaimed.

"I want him back!" Baby Frank cried. "Get him back for us, Jo."

It wasn't often that Baby Frank cried real tears, as he was doing now.

Josie put her arm around him and tried to comfort him. "I will, Baby Frank, if I can. Don't cry. Go on outside now, both of you, in case somebody returns Prancer."

As soon as she was dressed, Josie hurried out to the sidewalk where the boys had left the rocking horse the previous evening. She couldn't resist telling them that they should have taken better care of their toy.

"Maybe this will be a lesson for you," she said severely. "After this, put your things away at night."

"*You* didn't even want us to keep him!" Alexander pointed out. "Remember? You said you were going to put him out for trash."

"I was only fooling," Josie replied. She decided she would try to make up to her brothers by doing her best to find the rocking horse.

Alexander didn't want to lose any time, so he and Baby Frank, without waiting for breakfast, ran off to look for the man who had asked them all the questions the day before. He—and Josie, too—had decided that the man must have come back during the night and taken Prancer. Who else? Before the boys left, their sister managed to extract from them a very sketchy description of the stranger.

"He was tall and kind of thin," said Alexander.

"No, short and kind of thin," Baby Frank contradicted.

"Well, he was tan with blue eyes—"

"No, he was tan with brown eyes," said Baby Frank.

"Oh, shut up, you!" Alexander scolded. "You don't even know what colors there are."

"He didn't wear glasses," Baby Frank offered.

"No, he didn't wear glasses," Alexander agreed.

"I'm glad you're together on one thing," Josie commented. Her picture of the man was vague, to say the least, but that didn't stop her from deciding to search him out.

Shortly after the boys left, she departed for Eleanor's, to get her new friend to help. Although she felt sorry for her little brothers, she couldn't help thinking that this promised to be a new and completely unexpected adventure.

7

The Search Begins

Eleanor had not finished washing the breakfast dishes when her exciting new friend arrived. John Edward was caught foursquare when Josie met him at the back door just as he was about to leave. She immediately introduced herself and kept up a running conversation, ignoring his reluctant, short answers to her remarks.

"Eleanor!" he shouted at last. "Here's—" He stopped, and Josie realized that he hated to use the familiar name, but what else could he do? "Josie. She's waiting for you!"

"Don't hurry on my account, Eleanor," she called out blithely. "Your big brother and I will be getting acquainted."

Eleanor came quickly then, as if to the rescue, and John Edward, with a muttered explanation, unclear to anyone but himself, clattered down the back porch steps and disappeared around the side of the house.

"Don't mind him," Eleanor explained to Josie. "He

doesn't like girls much, especially gabby—" She stopped in confusion, and Josie graciously pretended not to notice.

"He *is* cute, Eleanor," she remarked. "You said he wasn't."

Eleanor raised her eyebrows. "Did I?" She changed the subject, which plainly did not interest her. "I have to finish my work before I may go with you."

"That's all right. I'll wait," Josie replied, taking a chair. "Oh! I forgot! The rocking horse was stolen last night. Alexander and Baby Frank are fit to be tied."

"What!" Eleanor exclaimed. "Stolen? How do you know?"

"Well, it was missing this morning. They left it outside on the sidewalk last night, and that's what happened. It's gone."

"Poor Alexander and Baby Frank!" Eleanor said sadly. "They thought so much of that rocking horse. What are they going to do?"

"Oh, they've already left to hunt for the man. The one who had asked them questions yesterday. They think he came back last night and took it."

"It does look that way," Eleanor admitted.

"Yes," Josie agreed. "They gave me a description of him, and I thought maybe you and I could search for him, too. We'll go back to the Y tomorrow. That will keep. And the other places, too."

Eleanor nodded. "I'll hurry up with my work, so we can get started. Come in with me while I finish drying the dishes, and tell me what that man looked like."

"Don't hurry on my account," she called blithely. *"Your big
brother and I will be getting acquainted."*

There was no one else around the lower floors in Eleanor's house this morning. Her gramma and Aunt Marie were housecleaning in the attic. "They start at the top and work down," she explained to Josie. She repeated, as Josie followed her into the kitchen, "What did that man look like?"

"Well," answered Josie slowly, "he was about medium height, with medium brown hair and a sort of round, square face. He wasn't fat, nor thin. Just—medium."

Eleanor stared at her. "He sounds awfully—medium."

"Yes, I know," admitted Josie. "But do you know, Eleanor, I formed a picture of him in my mind as soon as the boys described him. I'm sure I'll know him."

Eleanor nodded, but didn't look satisfied. However, she hurried through her morning chores, swept only the middle of the kitchen floor, and merely touched the furniture with her duster.

"Aunt Marie! Gramma! May I go now?" she called upstairs when she had finished.

"All right," Aunt Marie answered. "Be home for lunch."

"I will. Come on, Josie."

As the two girls passed through the kitchen, Eleanor stopped suddenly. "Did you have breakfast?" she asked.

"Oh, no," replied Josie matter-of-factly. "We didn't have time, after we discovered the rocking horse was missing."

"None of you? The boys neither?"

"Uh-uh. They rushed right off, as soon as they could."

Eleanor looked as disapproving as her gramma would, Josie thought. She hunted around for something edible. "Here," she said, "have a peach."

"Thanks. Could I take one for Alexander and Baby Frank, too? In case we run into them?"

"Of course," said Eleanor. She raised the lid of the cake plate. "There's some chocolate cake left from last night," she remarked. Hurriedly, she wrapped the fairly large piece and stuffed it in her pocket.

"Which way should we go?" she asked as she and Josie went down the front steps to the street.

"The boys headed toward town because they saw the man walk that way yesterday," Josie replied. "How about if we go in the opposite direction?"

"All right," agreed Eleanor. "We can go around St. John's School and back through town."

After a few minutes of fast walking under a blazing sun, the girls began to pant.

"Phew!" exclaimed Josie. "I hope we find him soon. I'm hot!"

"What will we do when we find him?" Eleanor asked.

"Don't worry about that," replied Josie confidently. "Just let me see him once. I'll know what to do."

But as the pair hurried through streets that became more and more crowded nearer the business part of the city, Eleanor began to lag.

"Josie, I've already seen a dozen men who might have

been the one," she said. "Do you know what he was wearing?"

"Tan shirt and pants," Josie answered. "At least I think. Alexander and Baby Frank were a little mixed up."

They were on Green Street now, passing the public school building that housed the swimming pool. The same officer was on duty outside, and he raised his hand in greeting.

"Hello, girls! Back for a swim?"

"We don't have time today," Josie explained. "We're pretty busy."

He nodded as they hurried past him.

A few minutes later, while the two friends circled the school, Josie saw what she was looking for and let out a scream. "There he is! That's him!"

A man—medium sized—wearing a tan shirt and tan trousers, was walking on the other side of the street, in the same direction as that in which the girls were headed. He was about half a block ahead.

Josie took off, darting across the street, leaving Eleanor behind.

"Hey!" the policeman called as two cars screeched to a sudden stop to avoid hitting Josie. "Hey, young lady! Come back here!"

Josie paid no attention, but ran until she caught up to the man. Then she grabbed him and yelled, "Where is it? Where is it?"

The man looked startled, and tried to shake her off,

but Josie held on tighter. He wasn't going to get away from her!

Josie heard running footsteps behind her and knew that the policeman was coming. The man saw him and seemed relieved. He called out, before Josie could say anything, "Officer! For Pete's sake, find out what's the matter with this kid, will you? She landed on me like a wildcat."

"Where's the rocking horse?" Josie demanded fiercely, hanging on. "Just tell me that. What did you do with it?"

"Rocking horse?" The man looked bewildered. "I don't know what you're talking about."

"All right, young lady." The officer lifted Josie away from the man, then firmly held her arms. "Now what is this all about?"

"He took my little brothers' rocking horse!" Josie exclaimed. "Last night. He came around asking questions yesterday, and last night, he—"

"I tell you," said the man firmly, "I don't know anything about any rocking horse. Gosh, I haven't even *seen* one of those things in years. What would I want with a rocking horse, anyhow?"

Josie began to experience a sinking sensation.

Eleanor, who had followed the policeman as quickly as she could, looked scared. "Josie," she urged, "we'd better go."

Josie, staring at the two men, who were now facing her together, realized that she had been too quick. Again! She started toward Eleanor.

"Wait just a minute," commanded the police officer. "Let's get to the bottom of this. Did you *see* this man take your rocking horse?"

"No-o," Josie had to admit. "But my brothers did—I mean they saw him when he was asking all those questions about it. And they described him to me—"

"Did they *see* him take it?"

Josie didn't answer. She looked desperately at Eleanor.

"Well?" demanded the officer.

He had been so nice yesterday, Josie thought, stopping traffic for them and everything. Now he looked so stern she was almost afraid of him. And she was silly to try to find someone from Alexander's and Baby Frank's description. Those two—nitwits! Uneasily, though, she realized that she was blaming them for her own foolishness.

Unexpectedly, the victim of her impulsiveness came to her rescue.

"Never mind, Officer," he said. "She's all mixed up. Crazy little kid," he added kindly. "I have one of my own."

The policeman nodded. "All right, if you say so." Then he spoke to Josie sternly. "The next time you'd better be sure you know what you're talking about."

The girls walked away. *Slunk* was more like it, Josie thought.

"I was so sure he was the one," she explained to Eleanor. "He was just exactly what I imagined, after I heard the boys' side of it."

"Maybe your imagination is too—too strong," suggested

Eleanor. "Being an authoress and all, I mean," she added quickly. "Naturally."

Josie nodded. "Positively. That's true. I can imagine just about anything I want. Most of the time it's a good thing. *You* know. But today—well, I was wrong, I guess. Do *you* think so, Eleanor?"

Her friend, looking unhappy, inclined her head.

Josie stopped suddenly. "I'm going to apologize to that man. Wait a minute." Before Eleanor could say another word, she ran back to where the officer and the man were still standing. She said loudly and clearly, "I apologize. I made a mistake and I'm sorry."

The men looked surprised, then laughed good-naturedly. "That's all right," the stranger said.

Josie left quickly, before either of them could say anything more.

"I feel better now," she announced as she and Eleanor walked home. "It's always good to admit it when you're wrong."

Eleanor agreed.

Back on Delaware Avenue, Alexander and Baby Frank were sitting on the curb, looking dejected. They hadn't had any success, either, in the search, but at least *they* hadn't managed to get into trouble, Josie thought humbly, and was glad to offer them the peaches she had saved. Eleanor removed the chocolate cake from her pocket, and, although it was a sticky mess by this time, Alexander and Baby Frank wolfed it down.

Then Eleanor went home for lunch. She didn't want to be late, she said, and be scolded. She didn't say so, but Josie knew her friend felt that they were in enough trouble already.

8

A Likely Suspect

After lunch, Josie looked out of her kitchen window and saw that Eleanor had returned. "I'm here," she called. "Come on in."

The boys were still sitting on the curb, talking about the rocking horse.

Hot as it was, Josie had decided to bake peanut-butter cookies and had turned on the gas oven in the kitchen. Perspiration rolled down her face as she vigorously stirred the ingredients, then dropped spoonfuls of the dough on a battered old cooky sheet. She had just eased the whole batch into the oven when shouts from the boys startled her and Eleanor.

"Now what's up?" Josie asked, running to the window.

Eleanor was right behind her.

"Oh! Oh!" Josie exclaimed when she saw what was happening outside. "Here we go again!"

"My goodness!" Eleanor gasped.

This time, the boys had captured someone—a medium-sized man wearing tan trousers and a tan shirt—and they were clinging to him like leeches.

"We'd better get out there," Josie declared, turning from the window. She hurried through the kitchen, and jumped down the back steps, closely followed by Eleanor.

"Alexander! Baby Frank!" she called sharply. "Come back here. Leave that man alone." Forgetting her own earlier impulsiveness, she now became the wise older sister, checking the boys' actions.

"But he's the one!" shouted Alexander, grasping the man's arm with both hands. "He's the one who took our rocking horse!"

Baby Frank, meanwhile, had wrapped himself around the man's legs.

"He took our rocking horse!" he chanted. "Took our rocking horse."

The man was half-laughing, half-indignant. He was trying vainly to detach the boys from him, but as soon as he loosened Baby Frank and turned to Alexander, the younger brother was back on his legs again. Finally, he gave up. "I'd have to have four hands to pry you off." He appealed to the girls. "Can't you do something about these two?"

"Here, kids!" Josie directed. "Let go! He isn't going to run away. Let go, I say!" she repeated fiercely, going over and dragging Alexander bodily away from the man.

Eleanor managed to clutch Baby Frank and hold him.

"Now," said the man, free at last. "First, let me tell you this right off. I don't have your rocking horse. If it's gone —*I* didn't steal it."

"You were asking us all those questions about it," Alexander blurted.

"Yes," the man admitted readily. "My name is Pippit,

by the way. Yes, I was asking about the rocking horse. And I would have bought it. That's why I came around now, to see if I could talk to your mother or father."

A smell of something burning floated through the kitchen windows.

Josie shrieked, "My cookies!" and tore away.

Everybody—even Mr. Pippit—waited anxiously until she reappeared, holding the blackened cooky sheet on which reposed the charred remains of the peanut-butter cookies.

"They're ruined," Josie said mournfully. "Every one."

"Oh, that's too bad," Mr. Pippit declared sympathetically.

Josie dumped the cookies—sheet and all—into the garbage pail by the back door. "That's that," she said. Then she looked up. "You said you wanted to *buy* our rocking horse?" She frowned. "Why would you want to buy that old thing?"

Mr. Pippit hesitated. "Well, I believe it is an antique, a relic of the Bonaparte estate—down in Bordentown, you know," he explained. "It answers the description of such a rocking horse that was the plaything of Joseph Bonaparte's grand-nephews. In that case, it would be valuable—very valuable. I was willing to pay for it—pay well, too. Antiques are sort of my hobby. But I have no designs on your rocking horse, fellows," he continued earnestly, "except to buy it, and only if you all agreed."

He sounded so convincing and looked so concerned that the entire group was impressed—even Baby Frank, who at first turned uncertainly to Alexander, then followed his big brother's lead.

In fact, Josie thought, Mr. Pippit was a nice man. His blue eyes were kindly, and his face, which was neither young nor old, just about medium, was attractive and friendly. She couldn't help liking him. She was sure he hadn't taken the boys' rocking horse.

But it was his explanation that was so amazing. She could hardly believe it.

"A *Bonaparte* rocking horse?" she asked. "Why, that was Napoleon's brother, wasn't it—Joseph Bonaparte who came to Bordentown?"

Mr. Pippet nodded. "Yes, he lived there for over ten years. Built a big house with acres of gardens, running right down to the river. Summerhouses, and underground tunnels, and children's dollhouses all over the grounds. He had been king of Spain, you know, before he escaped to America, and he continued to live like a king over here on his estate, Point Breeze."

"Napoleon's brother. Imagine it!" exclaimed Josie, still shaken by this news. She sank to the ground and gazed off into space. "And *we* had his rocking horse."

Now she saw Prancer in a different setting—on a smooth green lawn overlooking the river. She remembered pictures she had seen of Point Breeze, in some old history book. She could recall the engraving now, and a calmer, more placid, and contented scene would be hard to imagine. Little children dressed in long satin trousers and tight jackets, or full-skirted dresses, dotted the landscape.

Prancer—only he wasn't Prancer then. He was probably known by a grander name, like Roland, or Charleroi, or maybe Chevalier—must have been there, too.

Alexander brought her back to reality. "But *somebody* took Prancer," he insisted. "And we want him back. To keep ourselves. We're not going to sell him. We like him."

Mr. Pippit nodded again. "I'm beginning to understand how much you think of the rocking horse," he said. "And if you feel that way, it's all right with me. I'd like to help you get it back, though."

"Somebody took it on purpose," Josie declared.

"Yes," Mr. Pippit agreed. "I think so, too. Someone must have been around here and seen the toy, maybe even heard me asking about it."

"Think, Alexander!" exclaimed Josie excitedly. "Who was around then? When Mr. Pippit was here?"

Alexander wrinkled his brow. "I can't remember."

Josie decided to investigate this case. "Now we've all got to remember," she began. "First of all, just when was it you were here yesterday, Mr. Pippit?"

"Let's see. About two, or two-thirty, it was. I had lunch at home—I live over on Olive Street—because I'm on my vacation now. I work in Stern's Department Store. And it was—"

"Those guys were around!" Alexander exclaimed suddenly.

"What guys?" Josie demanded.

"You know. Those big guys who came by in the morning and we wouldn't let them pass—at first."

"They mean Mike Foley and Albert Schmidt," Eleanor explained.

Alexander nodded. "And a couple of other guys, and some old ladies, and some little kids—"

Baby Frank piped up. "And that tall skinny guy we beat up that day—"

Alexander turned fiercely on his little brother. "Shut up," he muttered, glancing sidewise at Josie.

Josie was puzzled. But Eleanor clapped her hand to her head. "Tom Willis!" she blurted.

"Who?" demanded Josie.

Eleanor explained. "John Edward told us at home that he saw Alexander and Baby Frank in a fight with Tom Willis."

Josie remembered now the conversation she'd overheard at Eleanor's house.

Alexander was glaring at Eleanor. Josie knew he preferred to keep his and Baby Frank's battles a secret from her.

Eleanor evidently sensed Alexander's outrage and said quickly, "But it wasn't anything, really. Tom Willis is just a smart aleck. He wouldn't know an antique if he fell over one!"

Josie wasn't satisfied. However, Baby Frank distracted her by declaring, "Maybe Prancer's back in the dump."

"Don't be silly, Baby Frank," she said. She explained to Mr. Pippit, "That's where they found the rocking horse—at the city dump."

Mr. Pippit looked interested. "Did you tell anybody

else that's where you found it?" He added, "Maybe it's somebody's idea of a practical joke—if they *did* hear any of you say that's where it came from."

Josie winced as she remembered her own threats to put the rocking horse out for trash.

"I don't know," she answered and tossed her head. "*They*'re likely to tell anybody anything." She indicated her little brothers.

Mr. Pippit declared, "It might be worth taking a look. I'll get my car and drive down there." He started away, then called back, "I'll let you know if I see anything of the rocking horse—anywhere."

"Thank you," Josie said. "You've been a big help. Positively."

Mr. Pippit grinned and waved a good-by.

Alexander watched him go. Then he said to Baby Frank, "He's okay. I don't think he took our rocking horse—now."

Baby Frank agreed. "I'll bet you it was that guy we beat up. I saw him yesterday, standing across the street."

"Will you shut up about that?" Alexander muttered. "Come on, let's get back to the yard."

The girls waited until the little boys were out of sight. Then Josie turned to Eleanor. "Now what's this about Tom Willis? The boys know something and Alexander won't let on. That's because I said I'd tell Mother if he got into any more fights."

Eleanor nodded and explained that Tom Willis had started the whole thing by making fun of the little boys' haircuts. That had angered them and they had attacked the bigger boy. Eleanor added, "But it was really self-defense. What right has Tom Willis to make fun of anybody?"

Josie declared, "He's the one, all right. If he was standing around here yesterday, he heard what Mr. Pippit was saying. Where can we find him?"

Eleanor hesitated. . . . "I don't know," she answered finally, looking uncomfortable.

Josie decided that Eleanor did know, but didn't want to say.

Her friend's next words confirmed this belief. "Tom Willis is mean," Eleanor asserted. "He's *always* making fun of people, especially smaller kids. And if Alexander and Baby Frank got the best of him the other day, he won't forget it. He'll try to get back at them."

"Well, that's just what he did already," Josie declared. "Now it's our turn." She chewed her lip. "We've got to *do* something," she continued impatiently. "Tell we what he looks like, if you won't help me find him."

"Oh, no," warned Eleanor quickly. "Remember this morning?"

"Shucks," Josie replied crossly. "I'm not going to stop him. I just want to *see* him, so we can be detectives and track him down. That would be fun," she added, looking sidewise at Eleanor.

Eleanor seemed to be weakening.

My goodness, Josie thought, how could anybody resist

the thought of being a detective, especially when it was to trap someone as nasty as Tom Willis?

Eleanor jumped up from the curb where she had been sitting with Josie. "I'm going home," she announced. "I have an idea. I'll let you know how it works out."

"Come back after supper," Josie called, "if not before."

As soon as she said that, she was surprised at herself. Imagine—she, Josie Delaney, marking off the time of day by anything as unimportant as regular meal hours. It must be Eleanor's influence. *Her* whole life, Josie thought, was divided into neat little compartments of time.

But Eleanor had gone off, agreeing to come back after supper.

Josie wondered how she could ever wait until then.

9

Bonaparte Park

Mr. Pippit, a bachelor, evidently didn't pay strict attention to the clock, either. He arrived at the Delaneys' in his battered old car—one of his favorite antiques—just about the time when Delaware Avenue families were cooking supper. Aromas of frying meat and potatoes, baking pies, and steaming coffee drifted out tantalizingly from various kitchen doors and windows, and were wafted through the back yards and alleyways.

Josie's mother had returned from work, and had just started to open the bags of food she had carried home with her.

"Anybody home?" called Mr. Pippit from the sidewalk.

Alexander and Baby Frank immediately appeared from behind their fortifications in the yard.

Josie brought her mother out to meet their new friend, and on the way, quickly explained the circumstances of Mr. Pippit's earlier visit.

"No luck at the dump, I'm sorry to report," Mr. Pippit began. "I suppose we could ride up and down the streets in the neighborhood, although I've been keeping an eye out and I haven't seen anything promising."

Mrs. Delaney, after hearing of the reason for Mr. Pippit's interest, marveled over the historic background of the rocking horse.

"Bonaparte Park!" she exclaimed. "I remember hearing about it when I was a little girl. We passed it once, too, but the gates were closed and we couldn't see much of the estate."

"You can see it now," Mr. Pippit told her promptly. "Want to? How about if you all pile in my car and I'll take you there."

"Hooray!" cried Alexander, and Josie gasped, "That would be goregous!"

Baby Frank scampered around his mother like a puppy. "Let's go, Mommy!" he begged.

Mrs. Delaney, looking interested, hesitated, but only for a few moments.

"Shall we go, Josie?" she asked. "I was just starting to get us some supper," she explained to Mr. Pippit.

"Positively, we'll go!" Josie declared. She knew her mother was just as anxious for the trip as the children were. Young and pretty Mrs. Delaney—much prettier than her daughter, Josie thought generously, although people always said they resembled each other—was always ready for the unexpected. *She* never insisted on a regular schedule for living—mealtimes were flexible, bedtimes movable. And that's just the way they all liked it, Josie told herself, loyal to her mother. Of course, she was a little bit hungry now. Then she had a brilliant idea.

"Let's bring our supper with us! Could we, Mother?"

The little boys crowed at this suggestion, and almost before Mrs. Delaney had asked Mr. Pippit if it would be all right for them to provide a little something to eat, *they* were stuffing food in a paper bag. Alexander found a loaf of bread, and Baby Frank climbed on a chair to reach the peanut-butter jar in the kitchen cabinet. He jumped down with it, and tossed it in the bag. Next he added some raw potatoes from the provisions his mother had just brought home.

Josie stopped him. "We don't have to bring *everything*," she said. "How would we cook these?"

They finally settled on bread and peanut butter only, and Alexander thought of a knife, fortunately. Then they all piled into Mr. Pippit's car, the two boys in front, Josie and Mrs. Delaney in the back.

The car was an open one, high off the ground, with a stately roof and black leather seats that looked as though they could stand anything. Alexander and Baby Frank slid around on the front seat, trying to look in all directions at once. They seemed to have forgotten, almost, the reason for their journey—until Baby Frank remembered and told his mother, "We're going to see where Prancer used to live!"

They enjoyed the breeze as they rode through the sweltering city streets. Outside the city, the air was cooler, and when Mr. Pippit turned off on a delightfully shady country road, Josie felt that they were in another world. The trees along the way looked timeless. They could have stood like this when the Bonapartes rode past.

Mr. Pippit brought the car to a stop before he turned again, this time into a narrower, more thickly overgrown road. "This is the entrance," he remarked. They drove slowly along avenues of elms and oaks, towering, topless. Squirrels ran up and down the tree trunks, rabbits scurried in the underbrush, and birds flashed bright colors as they swooped across the road ahead of the car.

Josie felt as if she had entered the forest of the Sleeping Beauty, and strained to see ahead, expecting at each bend of the road to come upon a castle. Even Alexander and Baby Frank were awed and silent.

"There are twelve miles of roads and bridle paths," Mr. Pippit said. "I suppose the bridle paths are covered over by now. But the deer still roam about. And we'll be able to see the lake when I stop."

"But where is the castle?" Josie asked.

Mr. Pippit smiled. "The house which Joseph Bonaparte built when he first came here burned down some years later. The only original building left is the lodge or gatehouse, which we passed at the entrance. Then Joseph built a second house—"

"Yes? Where is that?" Josie demanded eagerly.

"That, too, was destroyed, after the Bonapartes left America, by a rich man who bought the estate and had no love for its Napoleonic associations. He tore down

Joseph's house and built another. And that's the one we can see through the trees—in just a minute."

Josie groaned. She would never see the enchanted castle. It had disappeared long ago.

"However," continued Mr. Pippit cheerfully, "after we leave the estate, I can show you the very house in Bordentown where Joseph's nephew, Lucien Murat, lived. And that is where your rocking horse, if it is a genuine Bonaparte, came from, because Lucien married a Bordentown girl and his four children were born in the house on East Park Street. I have no doubt that the rocking horse belonged to them."

Josie felt better.

Then their car, moving slowly through the trees in the forestlike park, turned once more and stopped. Mr. Pippit waved a hand: "There is the house. It is a seminary now, and we can't go any closer."

They all peered at the long, rambling structure that was almost hidden by the trees. Beyond it was the river. The sun was setting by this time and the water seemed to glitter with golden light. They were all quiet, watching, although nothing moved, no person or animal stirred.

Josie sighed. "How gorgeous!" she murmured, because she couldn't say—out loud—the strange, other-worldly effect this overgrown green place had on her. Even the boys were quiet here.

"On to Park Street," Mr. Pippit said at last.

"And then home," Mrs. Delaney added. "It's getting late."

Alexander and Baby Frank remembered their picnic lunch, and, as the car left the park, they dug out the bread and peanut butter. Soon they were munching as they rode into Bordentown.

Park Street, when they reached it, turned out to be still, too, at this hour.

"They've made several small houses from Lucien Murat's former home," Mr. Pippit explained as they stopped before a mellow old building of cream-colored stucco. "This was a very big house originally. It was called Linden Hall."

"You certainly know a lot about the history of Bordentown, Mr. Pippit," Mrs. Delaney commented.

"Sort of my hobby," he replied modestly. "I used to live in Bordentown, you see, and when I was a boy, I played around on the estate. We kids used to love to go into those old caves—"

"Caves? What caves?" Alexander demanded.

"They are not really caves—just what's left of the old tunnels Joseph Bonaparte built to connect his house with that of his daughter, which was some distance away. On rainy days or in bad weather, the family used the underground tunnels to go from one house to the other."

"That's really exciting," declared Josie. "Imagine what you could do with an underground tunnel!"

"Those tunnels caused a lot of talk and stories," Mr. Pippit told her. "They used to say Joseph had them built so that if his brother, Napoleon, ever managed to escape to America, he could be hidden in them, in case of danger."

"Can't we see the caves?" Alexander asked.

"Not today," Mrs. Delaney said firmly, before Mr. Pippit could answer.

He went on to explain, "There's not much left of them. The tunnels have been filled in, mostly, except for some scattered places which the children of Bordentown called caves. I'm not rightly sure they're still there. But that's another trip—someday."

"I want to see those caves—soon," Alexander insisted, and Josie agreed eagerly.

"Tell you what," Mr. Pippit added. "When the fathers at the seminary open the place—as they do every year during the summer—for their annual picnic, we'll go and explore the caves."

"Do you promise?" Alexander demanded.

"I sure do," Mr. Pippit said, and patted the boy on the head. "I'll remember, sonny. To tell you the truth, I'm always glad to go back there myself. Reminds me of old times."

"And now I think we had better start for home," said Mrs. Delaney. "It has been a lovely ride, Mr. Pippit, and we've learned a great deal, besides."

"I'll never feel the same about that old rocking horse again," vowed Josie. "If we get it back, that is."

This doleful reminder caused Alexander and Baby Frank to howl.

"I want Prancer back," Baby Frank cried, and would not be comforted until his mother reached over and lifted him to her lap.

Alexander, being older, held back his tears. He merely swallowed hard a few times and stared straight ahead. "Let's start looking again as soon as we get home," he suggested.

"Wh—where?" sobbed Baby Frank.

"Oh—everywhere. Up Delaware and down Willow. Up Spring Street and down Summer Street. Up—"

"I think you should forget about looking for that rocking horse," said Mrs. Delaney. "I don't see what good it's going to do you to run up and down all the streets in the neighborhood, searching for it. You'll only get into more trouble."

Josie decided not to say one word. She didn't want her mother to forbid *her* looking for the toy, because she fully intended to do everything under the sun to find it. The journey to Bordentown had merely served to convince her of Prancer's value. She was mortified to think that only now, when it was lost, did they realize the rocking horse's worth. But a more reasonable thought comforted her a little. Maybe they wouldn't have learned all this about Prancer's connection with the Bonapartes if the toy hadn't disappeared.

"But, Mom," Alexander was saying, "Prancer was like a member of the family."

Josie suddenly realized that her motive in wanting to find Prancer differed somewhat from that of the boys.

They wanted their favorite plaything back—to keep. She wanted it back for another reason. Prancer would be very useful, to her mind, if he could be sold for a lot of money. How the family could use a lot of money! Her mother might even be able to give up her job before Pop was better and could come home—and support his family as he wanted so badly to be able to do.

But she decided not to upset the boys further by mentioning this. After all, they had to find the rocking horse first.

They were back in Bampton by now, and pretty soon back on Delaware Avenue, where, supper hour being over, people were sitting out on their porches and steps, trying to catch the evening breeze.

The Delaneys thanked Mr. Pippit, and he drove away, followed by the curious glances of the neighbors.

Mrs. Delaney waved and smiled to the nearest of them, and led her family inside the house which already, Josie thought, looked like *home*.

"We'll have supper now," her mother said. "And about time!"

10

Waiting It Out

That evening, after they had finished their delayed supper, Josie and her mother were sitting on the front porch steps when Eleanor returned. It was the first chance Mrs. Delaney had had to catch her breath, she said, since the family moved to Delaware Avenue—and the first time she had seen Eleanor.

Josie introduced her mother proudly, and was gratified by Eleanor's look of surprise, followed by one of admiration. Mrs. Delaney did look young enough to be Josie's older sister, as many people said. She didn't try to look young on purpose, either—in fact, Josie considered her mother to be very careless about her appearance. She never wore high heels, or fancy hair arrangements, or any of the other things Josie wanted her to try. But the dark hair waved naturally, the brown eyes crinkled with laughter, and the faded blue cotton dress became her as well as silks and satins did other people.

"Good evening, Eleanor," Mrs. Delaney said when their visitor was introduced. "What do you think of this family of mine?" She smiled warmly and moved over so Eleanor could sit between her and Josie.

"I like them," Eleanor replied earnestly.

"Good!" exclaimed Mrs. Delaney and patted Eleanor's hand. "That's one besides me, then."

"Do you know that we've only been here three days?" Josie asked. "It seems as if we've always lived in this house, though. I like it. So do Alexander and Baby Frank. They haven't been so happy in ages, with the whole corner to themselves."

"I think you should put a stop to that barricade business, Josie," said Mrs. Delaney. "The lady across the street told me about it."

"But, Mom, they have such fun thinking up a new password every day. Do you know what it was today? Wissinoming!"

Mrs. Delaney laughed and got up. "But they must not harm anybody bodily. Remember. Now I'll leave you two girls while I get some things ready for tomorrow."

"Your mother's nice," Eleanor told Josie as soon as Mrs. Delaney had left.

"I know," said Josie complacently. Then she turned eagerly to her friend. "Now tell me. I didn't want to ask in front of my mother, because she'd only say to forget about the rocking horse. But—what *was* your idea? Is it going to work out?"

Eleanor nodded. "I wanted to ask John Edward if he

would help. And he will! He says he'll keep an eye on
Tom Willis for the next few days."

"Oh, that's great!" exclaimed Josie. "Maybe he'll come
over here and report."

"No," Eleanor replied flatly, "he won't. I really had to
coax him to do anything at all. But he said he liked your
little brothers and he'd do it for them."

"Well, at least he's on our side," declared Josie, feeling
a bit let down. "Alexander and Baby Frank are out hunt-
ing for Tom Willis right now. I know they are, although
they didn't say so in front of my mother."

"I hope they don't get into another fight," said Eleanor. "And if Tom Willis did steal their rocking horse,
he'll have it hidden by now. He's pretty tricky."

"Mr. Pippit came back to tell us the rocking horse
wasn't at the dump. I never did think so, myself. Then
he took us all on a gorgeous ride, down to Bordentown,
and we saw where the Bonapartes lived. I was wishing
you were with us, Eleanor. After supper, I heard Alexander say to Baby Frank that it was time they followed up
the next clue."

"I hate to tell you this, Josie," Eleanor said, "but Tom
Willis just loves to break things up. He's always chopping
up old furniture and boxes for firewood, and then he
goes around selling it. Why, he even tried to sell
Gramma firewood after she'd given him an old table she
didn't want."

Josie had a horrible image of the boys' beloved Prancer

being splintered by an ax. "Do you mean he would *destroy* the rocking horse? On purpose?"

"John Edward said that's what he'd probably do," Eleanor answered unhappily. "Nobody would ever be able to trace it, then."

Josie moaned, "Oh, no!"

It was awful to think of such a calamity. That the old rocking horse should have weathered all the years from the Bonaparte era in Bordentown right up to the present —and now be in danger of destruction because some stupid boy wanted to avenge himself on the Delaneys was too awful. It mustn't happen! Josie jumped up.

"We've got to find this Tom Willis," she declared. "Prancer isn't going to end up in somebody's kitchen stove if I can help it!"

"But I told you, Josie. John Edward is going to watch Tom Willis. He can do it easier than we can. If he sees the rocking horse, he'll think of some way of getting it back. Don't worry," Eleanor tried to calm her companion.

Josie sank down again. "All right. I'll wait and see— for a little while, anyway." She pressed her hands to her head. "But it's hard when you're so anxious to do something!"

"Let's give John Edward at least a day—tomorrow," Eleanor suggested. "Then if he can't find out what has happened, we—"

"You and I will take over," Josie promised firmly.

She felt vaguely dissatisfied, though, and had to hold

herself back from trying to rush off in several directions at once, *doing* things. She wanted to see John Edward in person and give him some suggestions about spying on Tom Willis. She wanted to find out about the history of the rocking horse, and wished she had asked Mr. Pippit more questions. Above all, she wanted to get her hands on the old toy itself, examine it for any special signs of its having been owned by the Bonapartes. And she couldn't do any of these things!

Just then, Alexander and Baby Frank arrived back home, looking as frustrated as Josie felt.

"No luck?" she asked, although their faces told the story.

Alexander shook his head, and he and Baby Frank sat down on the curb under the street lamp on the corner, where clouds of flying insects fought each other in the light.

Eleanor left, declaring the mosquitoes were starting to bite.

Josie remained sitting on the porch steps, her chin in her hands. She wished she could forget the rocking horse. She'd made so many plans with Eleanor, and had looked forward to some interesting adventures in this new neighborhood. At first the search for Prancer seemed to promise some excitement. Now she couldn't rest thinking about what the family had lost—not the rocking horse itself so much, but its value. If it really was a historical relic of Bonaparte days, the toy must be worth lots of money. And surely the Delaneys needed money. They might receive enough for Prancer to put a down payment on this house. Josie was tired of her parents renting houses, and then having to move when the rent was raised, or when the family couldn't pay on time. This had happened a few times when some emergency—such as Alexander's hospital treatment for pneumonia last year —took all their available cash. And, of course, now there was her father's illness.

Yes, it would be nice to exchange the rocking horse— attached as her little brothers were to it—for something much more badly needed.

First, of course, they had to find Prancer—or Charleroi, or Roland, or whatever he was called in the old days of the Bonaparte residence in Bordentown.

Hardest of all, *she* had to sit still and wait patiently for twenty-four hours to pass, because she had promised Eleanor.

11

A Visit

Josie decided the next morning that she just couldn't sit idly by and wait for all those hours to pass. She had to be doing *something*.

Because the day was, if anything, even hotter than the ones before, she suggested to Eleanor that they try to take their minds off the missing rocking horse by going for a swim. It was Thursday, girls' day at the Green Street pool, so, provided with their bathing suits and towels, and the registration cards they would have to show, the two friends left Delaware Avenue early.

The officer who was stationed outside the school building recognized them, of course. Who wouldn't, Josie thought, after what had happened yesterday? He greeted them with a broad smile. "Find your rocking horse yet?" he called. Just saying "rocking horse" seemed to amuse him.

"Not yet," Josie replied, and added confidently, "but we will."

"Just look before you leap, next time," he advised.

"All right, all right," Josie muttered—but not loud enough for him to hear.

The girls continued on their way to the pool. They showed their registration cards before entering the locker room.

"Don't forget," Josie reminded Eleanor. "Your name is Carney, and mine is Johnson."

Eleanor nodded, looking worried. "I hope no one asks us."

Nobody did. The young lady instructor called them—and everybody else, "Hon."

Eleanor was content to paddle around the pool. Josie was more daring, and tried diving. This was harder than she had realized.

Afterward, the pair showered, dressed, and walked to the Y. Just as Josie had predicted, there was a different lady on duty, and the girls were ready with their new city identities. They were enrolled free for the junior cooking school.

Eleanor was looking very unhappy, and Josie knew her friend's conscience was bothering her. She didn't say anything, however, because the cooking school would not start for another week.

They wandered out to the street again, ready for the next adventure.

"I'm starving," Josie announced. "And I don't feel like going all the way back home for something to eat."

"What else can we do?" Eleanor asked. "Besides, they expect me home for lunch."

"Oh, they *always* expect you," Josie said rudely. "Can't you miss a meal at home just once? I never knew anyone who paid so much attention to being on time for meals. Gee, would the world come to an end if someone in your house missed lunch or supper?"

Eleanor was indignant. "And I never knew anyone who was so careless about meals. What's wrong with having a time for things? It's better than never having anything on time—like you!"

Josie felt herself growing angry. By a great effort, however, she held back another hasty retort. She stared straight ahead for a moment, until a side glance at Eleanor showed her friend looking scared and a little remorseful. Then, quickly, Josie turned all the way at the same moment that Eleanor decided to do the same thing.

"I'm sorry!" both girls said at once.

Then they burst out laughing.

Josie sighed in relief because her friendship with Eleanor had not been broken off. She referred to her earlier remark. "It *is* too hot to walk all the way back to Delaware Avenue," she began reasonably. "We were going to find out about tennis, remember? So why can't we just stay downtown and go over to the tennis courts this afternoon? It would save us a lot of walking."

Eleanor was silent.

"Say!" Josie exclaimed. "We just passed Ewing Street. Didn't you say your aunt or somebody lives there?"

"My great-aunt," Eleanor corrected her. "Gramma's sister. Mrs. Carney."

"Well," said Josie triumphantly, "let's go there for lunch. Why not?" she demanded as Eleanor hesitated.

"We don't go there very often."

Josie's puzzled frown seemed to demand an explanation.

"I'm not quite sure why," Eleanor continued. "I've never been to visit Aunt Winnie without Gramma, Aunt Marie, and maybe a few other people along. Aunt Winnie is—" She hesitated.

Josie, interested, helped out. "Forceful? Dominating?" She was pleased to be able to use some dictionary words in their conversation.

Eleanor shrugged. "I just never feel that I can manage her all by myself."

Josie immediately felt a thrill of anticipation. Although it would never occur to Eleanor to stop in and pay a casual visit to someone as intimidating as her aunt Winnie, Josie reacted differently. She was now curious to meet this Manning relative. "Why can't we both go?" she asked. "I'll be there to help."

Eleanor still hesitated.

"Besides," added Josie slyly, looking at her sidewise and grinning, "that's where you live now, anyway. Don't you remember? We might as well make it legal."

Eleanor didn't look any happier about this side of the visit, but she seemed to realize that she was losing the argument. In addition, all this time she had been walking with Josie back toward Ewing Street.

When they reached the corner, Josie exclaimed, "My goodness! I just wish I had an aunt who lived in a nice neighborhood like this."

They had been passing pleasant, semi-detached houses with shady front porches, awnings, and potted plants.

"There's Aunt Winnie's," said Eleanor. "Number 12."

"It's just as nice as any of the others," Josie declared.

"She's had that rubber plant ever since I can remember," Eleanor remarked. "She wipes the leaves with castor oil."

"Ugh!" exclaimed Josie. "How does she ever reach the top of it?"

The plant rose almost to the porch ceiling.

"With a ladder, I guess," Eleanor answered, and giggled.

Josie laughed, too, and led the way up the steps of Number 12. They stood, giggling together, while Josie pushed the doorbell hard.

Soon they heard a slow, heavy tread approaching. Then the door opened and an elderly woman, as thick and stout as a tree stump, and with just about as much expression on her face, stood before the girls.

"Well?" she demanded—and didn't sound very friendly.

"Good morning, Aunt Winnie," Eleanor said timidly, stepping forward. "I'm Eleanor."

"Oh!" exclaimed Aunt Winnie, and uttered a short sound that could have been a grunt. "I didn't recognize you." Still, she didn't ask the girls in. "And who's this with you?"

Josie didn't wait for Eleanor to explain. "I'm Josephine Marcella Delaney," she said. "Eleanor's friend. I live on Delaware Avenue, near her, with my mother, who works in the telephone office, and my two younger brothers, who are named Alexander and Baby Frank. I'll be attending St. John's School in the fall, with Eleanor, and I expect to be in the sixth grade."

Aunt Winnie didn't smile. Instead, she frowned. "Why are you telling me all this?" she asked suspiciously, never moving from her position blocking the doorway.

"Because you look like a lady who would ask about all those things," Josie replied daringly.

Aunt Winnie still stared, her prominent blue eyes expressionless, her pompadour of iron-gray hair as firm and immovable as herself.

"Do you want some lunch?" she asked suddenly.

"That's why we came," Josie told her.

Aunt Winnie gave a snort which actually sounded like a laugh. "Come in," she invited, and turned to lead the way. "I was just about to sit down myself."

Aunt Winnie's house was extremely neat and orderly, although somewhat depressing, Josie thought, with its massive, overstuffed chairs and dark carpets.

As the girls followed the short stout figure of Aunt Winnie to the kitchen, Josie gave Eleanor a poke and a wink.

"There's bread and cheese, and iced tea, and for dessert, boiled rice," Aunt Winnie said. "Sit down."

"Oh, it's gorgeous here," Josie sighed, looking around.

Indeed, the kitchen seemed to be the most cheerful room in the house. It was old-fashioned, of course, with a great cupboard extending all the way up to the ceiling, and a shapely, pot-bellied stove attached to the wall by a big round pipe. There was a table near one window, and, surprisingly, for Aunt Winnie didn't look like the type who would care for pets, a cage with a canary in it near the other window.

Josie immediately went over and started talking to the bird.

"Well?" she demanded—and didn't sound very friendly.

"His name is Dickie," Aunt Winnie stated, setting out plates for her visitors.

"Naturally," said Josie. "All canaries are named Dickie."

Before the lady of the house could express her outrage at this remark—and she looked as if she were about to—Josie stepped to the other window. "Look, Eleanor, isn't this a gorgeous back yard?" she asked, pressing her face against the screen. "Just look at those flowers. You must have a green thumb, Mrs. Carney."

Aunt Winnie looked pleased. "Things do grow for me," she admitted. "Come on, now, sit down. I hope you like boiled rice."

"I *love* boiled rice," Josie exclaimed, "with sugar and cinnamon and lots of cream!"

Aunt Winnie really did smile—a little—this time. "That's just the way I like it myself." She poured iced tea into tall glasses.

"Is that mint?" Josie asked. "I've always wanted mint with my tea, but never had it before."

Mrs. Carney settled herself between the girls at the table. "Now," she said sternly, turning to Eleanor, "what have *you* to say for yourself?" Before Eleanor could reply, she continued, "How's your grandmother? And all the rest of you? I thought maybe you were all dead and buried over there, for all I've heard from you lately."

Eleanor gave an account of the Mannings—helped considerably by Josie, who confided, when John Edward's turn came up, that he was the handsomest boy she'd ever seen. This remark really caused a change of expression— almost a twinkle—in Aunt Winnie's eyes. Pretty soon, Josie found herself telling her hostess about the rocking horse and all the excitement since its disappearance. And, remarkably enough, Aunt Winnie listened—for quite a while—and she looked interested, too.

However, when Josie finished, out of breath, Aunt Winnie merely looked at her, hard, and said, "Well, well."

Josie decided she wouldn't bring up the subject of her—and Eleanor's—city names and addresses just now. No use trying Aunt Winnie too far.

After a while, she consulted Eleanor's wrist watch and saw that it was almost one o'clock. "We'll have to go," she declared, rising. "Thank you for a lovely lunch."

"Come back again," Aunt Winnie said surprisingly. "You hear, Eleanor? Come again, and bring this Josie with you."

Walking toward the tennis courts, after they had left Ewing Street, Josie remarked, "I thought she was very nice. I'd go every day if I had a great-aunt like that."

Eleanor, looking a little confused, said, "With you along, Aunt Winnie didn't seem so bad."

"She's not bad at all," declared Josie. "Just lonely."

At the tennis courts, which a large sign proclaimed were county-owned, Josie had to stop and figure out which names they would use.

"We can use our own names," she decided finally, "because this is county, not city. Unless," she added, almost longingly, "you'd care to think up some interesting new names. I kind of like that. Don't you?"

"We'd better not, if we don't have to," Eleanor said. "I'd rather be myself."

Josie was able to practice her powers of persuasion in convincing the young man in charge of the courts that she and Eleanor couldn't possibly provide themselves with tennis balls and rackets. Didn't *he* have some they could borrow? Reluctantly, the young man searched and was able to find two tired rackets and a few limp balls.

"You're supposed to bring your own," he told the girls. "These are old ones somebody just left here."

"They'll do," Josie declared. "We're just learning."

Today, there were only a few others using the courts, so the young man came over to watch the girls in their fumbling attempts to play tennis. Pretty soon, almost as if he couldn't help himself because they were such terrible players, he began to give them pointers, advice, and, finally, demonstration. Before they left, they were calling him Bud, and he was calling them by their first names.

As the two girls walked home at last, Josie declared she was highly satisfied with the day's events. What's more, she hadn't thought of the missing rocking horse more than a half-dozen times during all those hours.

Eleanor agreed until she reached her house. Then she remembered that she hadn't been home for lunch. Her aunt Marie was sitting on the front porch, waiting.

"Where have you been?" were her first words, spoken

with an unaccustomed frown. "We were looking all over the neighborhood for you. John Edward went over to Josie's, and there wasn't a soul around the place. And nobody knew what—"

Eleanor began to explain. Josie tried to help, feeling guilty. As soon as the name of Aunt Winnie was mentioned, Eleanor's grandmother came out to the porch with her sewing basket.

"If you'd only told us, Eleanor," continued Aunt Marie reproachfully. "Of course it was all right to go there—but who would have thought of that? And we were worried about you."

Eleanor hung her head, and Josie felt sorry for her friend.

Gramma, mending socks, looked up over her glasses. "Was it your idea to go to your aunt Winnie's?" she asked Eleanor.

"No—well, not exactly. Josie thought of it first."

Gramma nodded. "Uh-huh." Then, suddenly, a twinkle came in her eyes. "I imagine Winnie was struck with surprise."

"It seems to be Josie's ideas all the time," Aunt Marie remarked, and Josie became alarmed. She was not a good influence on Eleanor—that's what the aunt was thinking.

Eleanor seemed to sense this, too, and she exchanged a quick glance with Josie. "Please, Gramma," she begged, "I'll always come home on time after this."

Josie chimed in. "It was my fault. I won't let it happen again. I promise."

Gramma turned to Aunt Marie. "Shall we give them another chance?"

Josie, looking eagerly from one to the other, saw Eleanor's aunt hesitate, then smile and nod. "I suppose so," she said. "But the next time—"

"We'll remember!" the girls exclaimed together.

Josie promised herself that she would, indeed, no matter what she really thought about the fussiness of always being on time. She certainly did not want to lose Eleanor's friendship. That would be even more dreadful than the loss of her brothers' rocking horse.

12

On the Trail

Eleanor didn't return to Josie's until the afternoon of the next day. She hadn't received permission until after lunch, she told Josie, because of yesterday. She had bad news, besides.

John Edward had reported no success from his survey of Tom Willis's property. There was no sign of any rocking horse in Tom's back yard or in the alley next to it. Her big brother had even tried a bit of a trick, later, hoping to get a rise from Tom. Before some other boys, John Edward had mentioned, casually, that he had heard the rocking horse of those crazy little Delaney kids was worth a lot of money. Tom didn't seem impressed at all. "I don't think he has the thing," John Edward had concluded. "I would have seen the gleam in his eyes when I spoke about money."

Josie listened intently as Eleanor told all this to her. The girls were sitting on the Delaneys' rickety front porch steps, munching some cookies that Eleanor had brought.

"You know, Josie," confessed Eleanor, "I'm afraid Tom has already broken up the rocking horse—since he's mostly interested in firewood."

"But if he knows it's worth money," Josie argued, "he'll think twice before breaking it up."

Eleanor hesitated. "Maybe he never had it at all. John Edward doesn't seem to think he did."

Josie said decidedly, "*I* do. Who else?" She looked at her friend sharply. "It's up to us now. Much as I like your brother, Eleanor, I never felt that he—nor anyone else— could really take the same interest in this as we do. He's willing to be put off. But not me. I'm *determined* to find that rocking horse. I'd like you to help, Eleanor, but you must be certain, too."

Eleanor seemed doubtful. Josie thought she was probably remembering how certain *she* had been when she tackled that strange man downtown, demanding the rocking horse.

She tried to settle these doubts. "Now, listen, we've eliminated everybody else who was around and might have seen it. Mr. Pippit is out. Those friends of your brother's—Mike and Al what's-his-name—they're out. Or do you suppose *they* took it?"

"Oh, no, no!" Eleanor replied hurriedly. "They wouldn't."

"Well, the only other one the boys noticed was this Tom Willis."

"But other people—lots of them—passed by," Eleanor objected.

"Old ladies and little babies," Josie said scornfully. "The insurance man and the paper boy. How could they take it?"

"It was stolen during the night," Eleanor pointed out. "They could have come back."

Josie shook her head. "Why? Nobody ever thought twice about that thing until Mr. Pippit said—overheard by the guilty party—that it was valuable. And besides," she concluded triumphantly, "Tom Willis is the only one—so far—who has a reason to get back at the boys. They had a fight with him, remember?"

"Yes," Eleanor admitted.

"*You* said he was mean and tricky. *You* said he was always picking up old pieces of wood and furniture and stuff. *You* said he sold whatever he could—for money. So—what more do you want? He's our man!"

"All right," Eleanor agreed, convinced at last. "I guess he is. But what are we going to do about it?"

Josie got up and paced the sidewalk restlessly. "Lots. We'll shadow him and follow him and spy on him. We're bound to see him do something with the rocking horse eventually."

"He's bound to see us, too," Eleanor said. "And I'd rather he wouldn't. I don't like him."

"Haven't you ever read any mystery stories?" Josie demanded impatiently. "They call it 'tailing.' You don't tail someone so's he can see you. The whole point is not to be seen—but to know where he is every minute of the time."

"But how?" Eleanor asked.

"You duck in doorways and alleyways while you follow him, in case he turns around and sees you, and if he does turn around real quick and spots you, why, then you're looking in store windows, or tying your shoelace, or something. You just don't stand there, watching him."

"Suppose there isn't any store window handy," Eleanor objected.

"Oh, there will be, don't be such a pessimist," Josie said easily. "Now it's three o'clock. Shall we start? You'll have to point him out to me first. I haven't even seen him."

"He's usually at the playground in the afternoons, teasing the younger children," Eleanor said. "It wouldn't be so noticeable if I pointed him out to you there."

"Let's go, then!" Josie exclaimed, starting off almost at a run, so that Eleanor had to hurry to catch up with her. On the way, Josie remembered to tell Eleanor that Mr. Pippit had stopped by again during the morning. He had become very anxious for news about the return of the rocking horse. He had also advised the Delaneys that the museum would be most likely to buy it.

"That is, if it's ever found again," Josie explained, "and if it's really an antique."

"Two big ifs," Eleanor said.

As it happened, identifying Tom Willis turned out to

be very simple. There were many children at the playground that day, and the girls saw Alexander and Baby Frank among them, waiting their turn at the hand bars. There was a big boy there, too—a tall, ungainly fellow, with an unpleasant grin. He was standing beside the bars, calling out scornfully when anyone faltered or dropped to the ground.

"I bet he couldn't do it himself," Josie remarked, watching him.

"That's Tom Willis," Eleanor said quietly.

"Oh, ho!" Josie exclaimed. "I might have known."

Just then, Baby Frank, who had been prancing up and down impatiently, got his turn. He grabbed the bars as well as some others twice his size had and started to swing himself forward, hand over hand. Tom Willis, who was standing too close, made a lunge as if to seize him. Baby Frank returned this by kicking out at Tom, striking him in the chest. It couldn't have hurt much because Baby Frank was wearing sneakers. But Tom's face darkened and an ugly scowl replaced his grin. He grasped Baby Frank's legs and would have pulled him down from the bars, except for Josie, who ran over to the big boy and struck him recklessly. She succeeded in breaking his hold on her brother.

Tom Willis turned immediately when he felt Josie's blows. He looked as if he were about to hit her back, then Josie saw him glance around. She was a girl, and there were many watching, so it wasn't altogether surprising that he hesitated to strike her—in full view of witnesses.

"Attagirl, Josie!" Baby Frank called, and continued swinging manfully to the other end of the bars. He didn't seem at all afraid of possible revenge from Tom. "That's my sister!" he shouted at the big boy.

Tom sneered at Josie. "Big Sister came along just in time," he remarked, tossing the lank hair out of his eyes.

"Go away," said Josie coldly, and turned her back on him. But then sensing a movement on his part, she wheeled quickly as he reached to grab her. She jumped backward and exclaimed, "Keep your hands off me! And stay away from my little brothers—"

"Says who?"

"—or you'll be sorry!"

"Oh, yeah?" said Tom. He kept standing there, grinning.

Baby Frank and Alexander, not at all bothered, had run off and nimbly boarded the revolving wheel.

Josie stood on guard, facing Tom, disliking his smirking expression more the longer she looked at it. Finally, she turned away from him. "I'd like to slap his face," she muttered to Eleanor as they walked off.

"Well, now you know him," Eleanor remarked.

"And I'll never forget him. Never!"

Eleanor wanted to leave the playground.

However, Josie, a safe distance away, wanted to keep an eye on Tom Willis. "We'll follow him when he leaves," she declared.

Eleanor started to protest, but Josie gestured to silence her friend. She forgot all about time, and meals, and the disapproval of the Manning family. She was intent only on keeping a watch on Tom Willis without his being aware of it. Accordingly, she kept darting around, seemingly paying no attention to him.

Eleanor stayed, partly because Josie cowed her into submission.

"We can't leave now," Josie whispered fiercely. "We've got to follow him."

Tom Willis hung around an unreasonably long time,

and Josie became restless as the afternoon wore on. She watched him as he strolled from one group to another, always the mocking bystander, never joining in any game.

Eleanor had just said, "Josie, I've got to leave," when Tom sauntered out the playground gates.

"Come on!" Josie exclaimed urgently. "After him!"

"But it's too late!" Eleanor protested.

Josie didn't answer because she was already out on the street. She didn't care what time it was. This was her chance. With one part of her mind, she knew that she was being mean to Eleanor. But she didn't have time to be sorry now. Later, maybe. Thank goodness her own mother never seemed to worry if Josie didn't show up for supper. She merely saved something in the refrigerator or the oven, and the rest of the family went right ahead with their meal.

For a moment, Josie lost sight of Tom Willis, who was some yards ahead of her. She grew frantic. Where could he have disappeared already? What kind of detective was she? Then she saw him again, lurking near a porch, and she dropped down and crouched behind somebody's trash can, as Eleanor ran up. She motioned her friend to follow her example.

"Where is he?" Eleanor asked as she hid, too.

"He just went down that alley," Josie replied. "It runs the same way as this street. I don't know which way he'll turn, so you will have to cover one end of the alley and I'll watch the other end. Just go down the street a block, and I'll go the other way. If he comes out on your side, wave to me, and I'll come. Hurry up, now." Josie gave her a slight push. Eleanor had no choice—at this important moment—except to do as she had been ordered. So she went. . . .

A little later, when Josie saw Tom emerging from the alley, continuing on in the same direction as Eleanor, she motioned in answer to her friend's beckoning and ran up to join her. The two of them followed their quarry, everything else but the pursuit forgotten.

13

Getting Close

Tom did not seem to know that he was being "tailed." He plodded on, head down, sometimes kicking at small stones that lay in his path. Once, he stopped and turned around suddenly, after there was a loud bang, like a collision of some kind, several blocks away. The girls stopped, too, and froze in their tracks. It was too late to duck or scramble for cover. They held their breath.

But Tom didn't seem to notice them, and soon he started on again. The pair followed, this time even more cautiously.

"Where can he be going?" Eleanor inquired anxiously. "He lives on Summer Street, and we've passed that already."

Josie shrugged. She was enjoying the excitement of the chase, and she would be disappointed if it ended too soon.

They were now approaching Green Street. A crowd of young people streamed out of the school building, holding or swinging bathing suits and towels. The afternoon swimming session was over. Tom disappeared among the others on the pavement, and for a few moments, Josie again lost sight of him.

"He's gone!" she cried as she strained to catch a glimpse of his lanky figure. "He must have gone inside!"

"He couldn't," Eleanor told her. "It's too late. They are all leaving now."

"Oh, there he is!" Josie sighed in relief. "He's just turning the corner. Come on!"

She hurried ahead, weaving in and out of the crowd still clogging the exit of the pool. Eleanor ran to keep up. They arrived at the corner just in time to see Tom crossing the street, half a block ahead of them. Josie started across, too, recklessly, forgetting to stay under cover. Eleanor called a warning to her, but even as she did, Tom disappeared in one of a row of little houses that lined the entire block opposite the school grounds. It happened so fast that, as soon as he was swallowed up, so to speak, Josie couldn't be sure of the house he had entered.

She stood, mouth open, struck by surprise. Then she looked back at Eleanor and demanded, "Did you see that? He ran right straight in, didn't knock or anything. He doesn't live there. What does it mean?"

Eleanor shook her head helplessly. "You'd better come back here. He may look out the window and see us."

"Out the window of what house?" asked Josie crossly as she rejoined her assistant detective. "Which one is it?"

"I don't know," Eleanor confessed. "I thought you did."

There was a big maple tree near the corner, on their side, and they stood under it, ready to hide at the first sight of Tom Willis.

"Now what?" Eleanor asked.

"We wait," Josie replied. "He's got to come out sometime. We might as well sit down on the curb."

The swimming crowd was thinning now. The officer whom Josie felt they knew almost too well by this time—and who recognized them at once—saw the two girls and waved them on.

"Time to go home, young ladies," he said as he left his post and passed them.

"Pretty soon," Josie answered, keeping her eyes on the houses across the street.

The last of the swimmers, trailing their towels, were almost out of sight. A rather unnatural quiet settled over Green Street. The shadows lengthened, and Josie saw Eleanor glancing uneasily around. She was probably worried about the time. The sun had retreated to the far end of the school grounds, and was almost ready to sink down under the fence, and disappear.

"It's late," Eleanor said, almost to herself. "I should be going home."

Josie knew, though, that Eleanor was going to stay as long as she did. This was more important than anything else either of them could think of right now. Josie's eyes wandered, and the familiar street somehow seemed strange to her, strange and oddly empty.

Suddenly, she sat up and Eleanor's head jerked around. There was a movement—slight, but apparent—on that almost motionless street. Josie fixed her attenion on the row of little dwellings opposite. Yes, the door of a house, almost squarely in the middle, was opening . . . slowly. The girls scrambled to their feet and plunged behind the tree, which was thick enough to shield them. Then, as they saw what was emerging from the doorway of the house, Josie put out her hand and gripped Eleanor's arm.

"Look!" she breathed.

A big cardboard carton was coming out first, and behind it, almost hidden by it, was Tom Willis, pushing. He guided the box very carefully down the steps, as if it were heavy, and finally was able to ease it gently to the pavement. Then he pressed against it, moving it ahead of him in the direction from which he had come.

Josie, in her excitement, was squeezing Eleanor's arm. "That's it!" she exclaimed. "He's got the rocking horse in that box!"

Eleanor nodded.

"What else could be in a box that big?" Josie continued. "We've got him at last!"

Tom was about opposite them now, making slow but steady progress. He never once glanced over in their direction. His whole attention was on the box.

"As soon as his back is turned, we'll rush up and surprise him," Josie continued, her eyes glued to what was going on across the street.

Eleanor started to object. "But suppose—" she began.

Josie jumped suddenly and pulled her along. "Now!"

Tom turned when he heard Josie's triumphant shout.

"Got you!" she cried, running in front of him, blocking his path. "Where are you taking our rocking horse?"

The big boy glanced disdainfully at the girls. "Oh, so it's you, Miss Busybody," he said casually. "Get out of my way, will you?"

"I will not get out of the way!" Josie's voice was rising, and a few people came out of their houses to see what the noise was about.

"You have my brothers' rocking horse in that box, and I am going to take it back. Don't try to stop me!" She flung herself on him.

Tom held her off, with that superior, maddening grin of his.

It crossed Josie's mind—very fleetingly, for she was hanging on to her tormentor desperately—that he didn't seem angry, or act guilty, nor even surprised that he had been discovered with the rocking horse. But her attention was on holding him.

"Eleanor!" she called urgently, "try to grab his other arm!"

More people came out of the houses now, and Tom smiled as if he were enjoying the attention.

"I would like to know what you think you're doing," he said, glancing around to make sure others heard him.

"We're going to make you open that box!" Josie declared loudly.

Tom shook his head. "Oh, no, you're not. Why should I open it?" He was pretending to be indignant, but he wasn't, really. He couldn't wipe the grin off his face.

A tiny bit of doubt shook Josie. He was not reacting as she expected. She wondered if Eleanor had noticed, and glanced quickly at her friend.

Tom took advantage as she unconsciously eased her hold on his arm, and shook her off.

"Here comes that policeman, Josie!" Eleanor cried.

Josie decided to open the box herself. But she was all thumbs, and couldn't manage it. She kept plucking at it, though, feeling hurried and desperate.

"What's this all about?" the voice of authority demanded, and she looked up to see the familiar officer staring at her in a very unfriendly way.

"Well?" he repeated as Josie did not reply.

Then Tom spoke. "I wish I knew what it is all about," he said smugly. "These two girls jumped on me, yelling and screaming, with some crazy story about a rocking horse."

"Oh, so that's it?" the officer said, looking wise. He was remembering, Josie thought. "That—again?"

"He has our rocking horse in that box," she declared. "Just make him open it and see."

The policeman looked at her for a long moment, glanced briefly at Tom, then back at Josie. "You have rocking horse on the brain. You accused a man just the other day of having it, and now you accuse this boy. Well, it's a simple matter to straighten out this time. How about opening your box, son, and let's see? Then we'll all be satisfied." He looked meaningfully at Josie.

"Sure," said Tom obligingly. "Be glad to."

Josie shot him a glance that, if looks could kill, would have finished him on the spot. "You've certainly changed your tune," she muttered.

Tom ignored her and made a great show of prying open the cover of the carton, taking much longer than was necessary. He gazed around to make sure that everybody present was watching. Then, when he had the flaps of the box loose, he quickly raised them all up at once, stepped back, and exclaimed, "There! See for yourself!"

They all crowded around to look.

The box was empty!

14

Defeat

Josie stared, first at the empty carton, then at Tom and the officer, finally at Eleanor.

Then she turned furiously on Tom. "You sneaky thing!" she cried. "You—you—"

Tom shrugged and looked helplessly at the policeman, and said, "I give up. They don't make sense to me."

The officer turned to Josie. "Now, young lady," he said sternly, "I think it's about time we put a stop to this. You may begin by telling me your name—you and your friend, there—and where you live. Then we'll see what this rocking-horse talk is all about."

Josie, still sputtering, didn't answer. Eleanor looked frightened and Josie realized that this was a terrifying experience for her—a policeman asking their names!

"I'm waiting," he declared.

Josie started to do as he had ordered. "Josie De—" Then she stopped as a new and disturbing thought came to her. Their names! They had adopted different names and addresses for the swimming pool, and this policeman was stationed there every day. If they gave their own names and addresses, he'd know they weren't supposed to use the pool.

How awful!

For a moment, she felt dizzy, trying to figure out—quickly—what was the best thing to do. She and Eleanor would have to agree, and they couldn't say a word—in front of all these people!

Josie shot Eleanor a warning glance and said quickly, "Josephine Johnson, 149 Monument Street."

When the officer turned to Eleanor, she, thank goodness, knew enough to follow suit. "Eleanor C—Carney," she said waveringly, "12 Ewing Street."

The policeman said, "I'll have to see your parents about this."

Josie thought wildly, Why, he's going to those addresses! And there won't be any Josephine Johnson on Monument Street! Then she pictured Aunt Winnie when a policeman came knocking on her door, asking for *Eleanor Carney.*

Eleanor covered her face with her hands. Josie hoped her friend wasn't going to cry. She thought furiously. She'd have to get the two of them out of this fix—and quickly. How? Oh, what could she do?

But she hadn't reckoned on Tom Willis.

"Hey! Wait a minute!" he shouted. "That's not right. Her name"—he pointed to Eleanor—"is Manning. I know her brother. And the other one is Delaney. I know her *brothers.*" He couldn't resist adding, even though it was out of character with the air of injured innocence he was trying to keep up, "They're even crazier than she is—if that's possible."

The officer looked puzzled. "Somebody's wrong," he said. Then he asked Josie suspiciously, "What did you say your name was?"

Josie glanced at Eleanor and shrugged. They had to face it, she wanted to say. Aloud, she replied, "Josie Delaney." Then she raised her head and announced in a clear, ringing voice, "Miss Josie Delaney. And this is Miss Eleanor Manning." She added, "We were only fooling before."

The officer slapped his book shut, looking disgusted. "Fooling is right. Well, that settles it. I believed you the other day. Thought you were mixed up, and there really was a rocking horse missing. Now I can't trust a word you say. Wrong names—wrong story."

"Wrong addresses, too," Tom added gleefully. "They don't live where they said. Ask them again."

The policeman glanced at the girls keenly. "*Where* do you live? I want the truth, now. I'll pay a visit to your parents."

Although Josie was sure she'd been in jams as bad as this before, she knew Eleanor hadn't. Probably her friend felt like sinking right down to the ground and disappearing through one of the cracks in the pavement.

The officer got out his notebook again and wrote down

the addresses that the girls, feeling ashamed and embarrassed, gave him. But he didn't ask Tom for his, Josie thought indignantly. That mean boy stood by, smirking and grinning, enjoying the attention of the crowd that was growing bigger every minute.

Josie stared at him angrily. "Why don't you ask for *his* name?" she demanded of the policeman. "And where he lives? It's not here—" She pointed to the house Tom had just left. "And what he's doing with that big empty box? And—"

"That'll do," said the officer. "I'm in charge."

But Tom couldn't resist taunting Josie. He muttered, "The better to fool you with, my dear."

She glared at him, then turned to comfort Eleanor. She knew her friend was feeling miserable. "Don't worry, Eleanor. I won't let him go to your house. It doesn't matter about me. I don't want to trouble my mother, of course, but she knows I'm apt to rush ahead when I shouldn't without thinking things out first. But I can count on her to understand—and, after this, I'll surely be more careful. And this isn't going to disgrace Alexander and Baby Frank. What do they care? Only for their rocking horse, of course. And this was all done for a very special reason."

Eleanor smiled weakly, but any smile at all was encouraging, Josie thought. Then her friend endeared herself further by explaining the reason for her worry. "They'll never let me play with you again!" she wailed.

"I'll explain," said Josie, as firmly as she could. They

couldn't be so mean, she thought. That would be the worst possible outcome of this whole business—losing Eleanor's friendship.

"And I'm going to be late for supper," Eleanor added, unnecessarily, Josie thought. "Very, very late. After they warned me, too."

The officer closed his book. He nodded to Josie, turned to include Eleanor in his glance, and said, "Come on. Home."

15

The End of the Trail

The girls started away with the officer. Josie was trying to appear unconcerned. Eleanor was drooping.

They had gone only a few steps when the door of the small house from which Tom had come, pushing his carton, opened suddenly and a man looked out.

"Hey, Tom!" he called. "What are you going to do with this here rocking horse?"

The sudden silence which stopped everybody short couldn't have lasted more than a few seconds. But it seemed to Josie as though they stood there for ages without a sound.

Then the meaning of the man's words sank in, changing everybody's expression.

"Glory hallelujah!" Josie shouted. She ran over to Eleanor and hugged her.

Eleanor smiled, then looked frightened again as she

pointed out four figures in the distance, hurrying toward them.

Josie recognized Mr. Pippit, John Edward, and, right behind, the small shapes of Alexander and Baby Frank.

The policeman turned slowly to face Tom. Before the boy could run away, as he fully intended, judging from the furtive way he glanced around, the big, solid man, without any lost motions, blocked his path. "Not so fast," he ordered firmly.

Tom's face looked very different now. The smirk was gone—replaced by a scowl. The bystanders' faces altered, too. Now Josie thought they looked friendly instead of hostile.

Meanwhile, John Edward and company were dashing ahead, getting closer and closer.

Only the little man who had called out from the doorway seemed unaware of the effect of his words on everybody. He continued, rather fretfully, "There ain't enough room in the hall for the confounded thing. I fell over it twice already."

The policeman said, "Let's take a look at that rocking horse. Bring it out here, will you, sir?"

"Sure," replied the man. "Hold this door open, one of you kids. I'll be glad to get rid of it," he remarked as he pulled the rocking horse through the doorway.

When Josie saw Prancer's faded appearance and his sad but noble expression once more, she felt a sudden stab of affection for him, although he looked even shabbier than he had back on Delaware Avenue.

The man continued, giving the rocking horse a final tug, "Tom promised he'd take it away if I got him a box big enough for it. So when he came just a while ago, I thought—"

But no more explanations were necessary as far as Josie was concerned. She was delighted, not only because Prancer was safe, but also because she had been right all along about Tom, and she had proved she was a good detective in tracking him.

The little man, who identified himself as Tom's uncle, kept on talking, although no one seemed to listen.

The rocking horse was no sooner on the pavement, surrounded by an interested group of spectators, before

Alexander and Baby Frank rushed up. They pushed through the circle and clasped their beloved toy. Then they both tried to climb aboard at once.

"It's Prancer, all right," Alexander declared, stroking the horse's neck. "Where was he all this time?"

"He had him!" Baby Frank shouted, pointing at Tom.

Mr. Pippit hurried over to the rocking horse, stooped quickly to look under it. Then he stood up and nodded to Josie. "The real antique," he said quietly. He began talking to the officer, explaining the whole thing.

The policeman seemed satisfied at last. "But why the wrong names and addresses?" he asked the two girls. "That only made things worse."

Josie stepped forward. As reasonably as she could, she explained. All the while her words of excuse were tumbling out, she knew, regretfully, that the brief, city-township series of adventures with Eleanor were at an end. The policeman didn't really have to warn her, as he did. "Don't try anything like that again." She knew.

After listening to her, the officer moved over to Tom and the boy's uncle. Now it was their turn for explanations.

"You're late for supper," John Edward informed Eleanor, as if, Josie thought, that was the worst trouble possible. He didn't even look at *her*. "Gramma's mad. She said she told you—"

"I know, I know," Eleanor said quickly. She shook her head. "I have an awful lot to explain."

"We've had a very exciting afternoon," Josie informed John Edward.

He glanced at her briefly but didn't ask for details.

Josie wondered how she could startle him into paying attention to her. "We're reformed characters," she began.

Eleanor took this very seriously and declared earnestly, "I've learned my lesson."

John Edward reacted at last. "Well, I hope so," he remarked. "I'm hungry. We were waiting supper for you."

Josie sighed. She'd heard the saying that the quickest way to a man's heart is through his stomach. Whoever said that must have known all about the John Edwards in this world.

They were all starting homeward, with Alexander and Baby Frank ready to drag Prancer, when Josie thought of something better. She ran back to Tom's uncle.

"Could we have the carton, please? It'll be easier to get the rocking horse back to our house." She glanced at Tom, still doing a poor job of accounting for his actions to the officer, and added meaningfully, "Where he belongs."

"Sure, sure," said the uncle obligingly. He didn't seem to hold any grudge against anybody, Josie thought. He was really much nicer than his nephew.

Josie pulled the carton after her, with her eyes on Tom. She kept watching him until he finally looked at her, scowling. Then she tossed her head and quickly turned her back. She'd had the last word. She hoped she'd never have another with Tom Willis.

Alexander and Baby Frank took care of Prancer. Watching them, Josie wondered how she would ever convince them to part with the toy. Money meant nothing to the little boys, of course. But money was very important to the family just now. And it would be, she thought ruefully, until their father was all well again and could hold a steady job once more.

Then a sudden wonderful thought came to her. Prancer would stay the same, but the little boys would not. In a year, maybe less, Alexander would grow out of childish things, and Baby Frank would follow, later. Sad but true. The rocking horse wouldn't always be her brothers' favorite companion, their most precious possession. So let them have it now. She was sure her mother would agree that the family could wait. Prancer could wait, too. And if he ended up in a museum, as Mr. Pippit said was most likely, they could all go to see him, any time they wanted.

She linked arms with Eleanor. "Well, that's that," she said with satisfaction. "What'll we do tomorrow?"

Mary Malone

was born in Lambertville, New Jersey. She has lived and worked most of her life in Trenton. She attended Trenton State Teachers College, Columbia University and Rutgers.

Mary Malone says, "There are a lot of libraries in Trenton, as it is the state capital, also the county seat of Mercer and the home of several colleges, so I've worked in many different kinds of libraries—public, state and institutional; then, for the past almost twenty years, in school libraries, which really suit me best. The school where I worked previously goes from kindergarten through ninth grade—and it was a wonderful proving ground for children's reading interests. I am now serving as "coordinator" of elementary school libraries in Trenton.

"I like to travel and try to do some traveling during every summer vacation. Recently, I went to Ireland, where I visited all the towns and counties whose names are engraved on the headstones in St. John's Cemetery, in Lambertville, my home town, which I used as a background for my first book, *This Was Bridget*." The natural, homey quality of this genuine grass-roots Americana story won for it the top place in the *Dodd, Mead Librarian Prize Competition*.